S. M. Webber has worked as a teacher and has brought up two children. She has also written *Her Story in Four Centuries*.

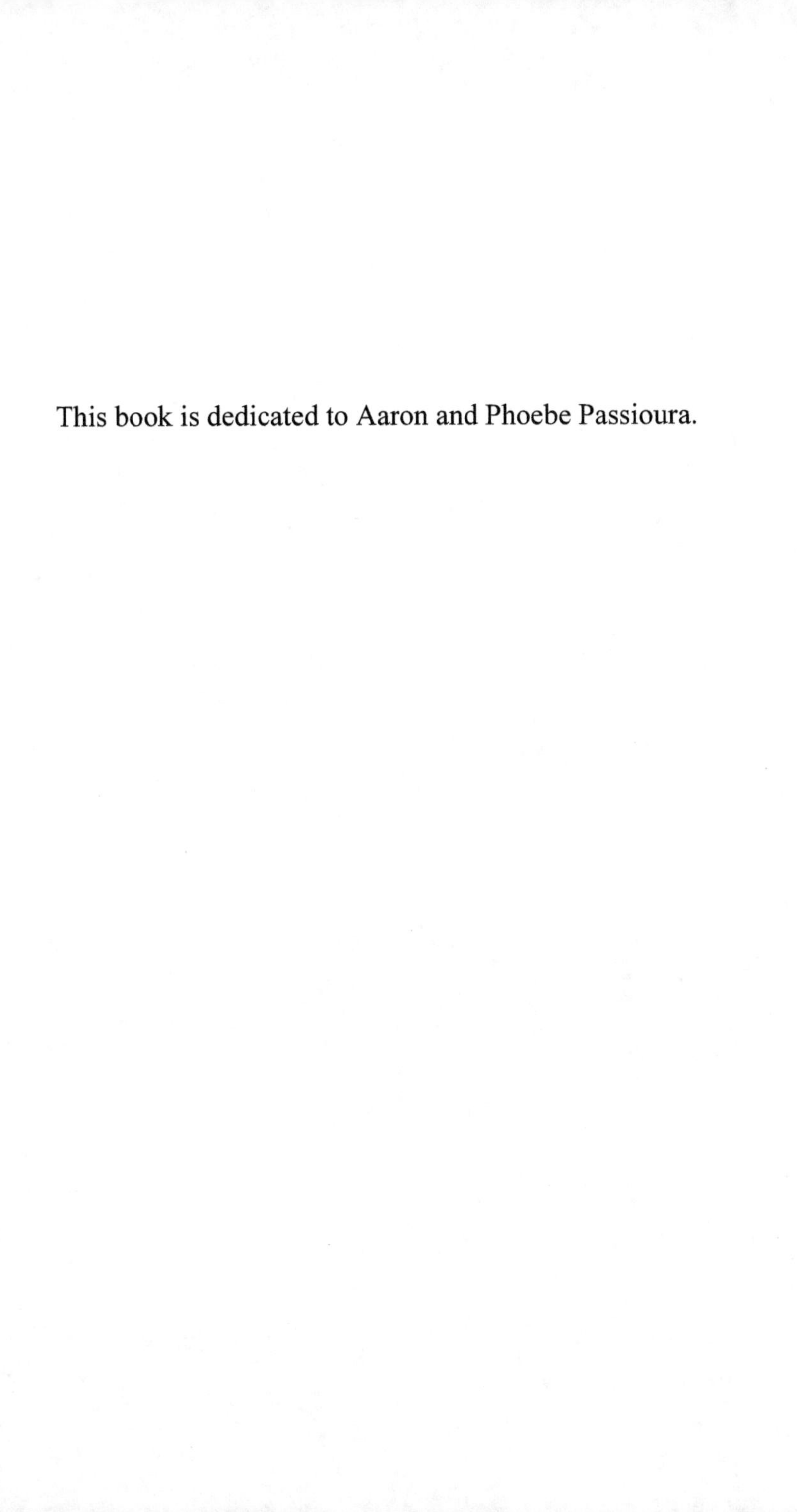

This book is dedicated to Aaron and Phoebe Passioura.

S. M. Webber

RIDER THE RUNAWAY

AUSTIN MACAULEY PUBLISHERS™

LONDON • CAMBRIDGE • NEW YORK • SHARJAH

Ordering Information:
Quantity sales: special discounts are available on quantity purchases by corporations, associations, and others. For details, contact the publisher at the address below.

Publisher's Cataloguing-in-Publication data
Webber, S. M.
Rider the Runaway

ISBN 9781643788159 (Paperback)
ISBN 9781643788142 (Hardback)
ISBN 9781645365266 (ePub e-book)

Library of Congress Control Number: 2020903013

www.austinmacauley.com/us

First Published (2020)
Austin Macauley Publishers LLC
40 Wall Street, 28th Floor
New York, NY 10005
USA

mail-usa@austinmacauley.com
+1 (646) 5125767

Thanks to my assessor, Tom Flood, for his critique,
and to Julian Cribb for his book, *The Coming Famine*.

The Blow-Up with Mum

Saskia was hammering in the nails on the weatherboard garage, which were tending to pop halfway out. *It's because it's old*, she thought. Sometimes, she glimpsed the name of her father, *Euie Smith*, that was cut into the handle of the hammer and recalled the photo of him, the severe lines of his eyes and mouth. Then she closed her fingers again and hammered harder. She was stuck at home for the summer holidays and there was nothing much to do in her small country town in Australia. *I wish Mum would come home so that we can go shopping.*

Mum had stayed overnight with Mark, her boyfriend. Saskia didn't want to phone when she was there, living a different life. She didn't like talking with Mark.

Suddenly, the hammer slipped from her grip and she smashed the glass in the small window at the back of the garage. Crash! Bits of glass splintering on the ground. *I'll have to pick them up.* She broke off all the glass so Mum wouldn't notice the edges and would think there was still glass in the window. For a long time, anyway.

The mobile phone rang.

"I'm running late. Mark is still finishing the work on my car. Are you all right?"

"Of course, I'm all right."

Much better at home alone, than staying at Mark's place being embarrassed as usual by their carrying on, kissing and cuddling.

But on her own at night, like last night, lying awake listening to the creaks and groans of the old house, she felt lonely and scared. She thought someone was climbing the stairs to her room in the attic. She huddled in the bedclothes. *I'm trapped!* Her heart pounded. Her brother, Peter, wasn't there as a buffer against boyfriends and burglars.

Mum had said that the trees and bushes were tapping on the house in the wind. They needed cutting back. Perhaps Saskia could do the job, she hinted.

Mum pulled into the driveway. "Goodness me, you look so dusty and untidy!" she called out, as Saskia walked towards the car. "I hope you're wearing clean socks for trying on new shoes."

"Yes, Mum," she said, brushing herself down with her hands. One hand was bleeding from cutting it on the glass.

"Well, hop in, and we'll go now."

Saskia slumped into the car seat. Mum backed out of the driveway and they headed for the shops. Saskia saw blood on her T-shirt and tried to hide her hand.

"I don't like you being away so much," she said. "I didn't have anyone to talk to."

"I told you to come too. You could watch the same TV shows at Mark's house. I was doing mending orders in the evening." She did dressmaking, mending, and alterations.

"No. All my things are at home. I wish you didn't have a boyfriend."

"Mark is a nice person. He helps us. He would have shown you how he was repairing the car."

Mum parked near the shoe shop and they walked in.

"Mark was bossing me around about cleaning up after myself. He's not the boss of me." She kicked the stand of shoes.

While Mum explained to the shop assistant what they needed, Saskia sat down meekly. She tried on the black leather shoes that he brought. "I don't like these 'sensible shoes'," she said to Mum. "I prefer the trainers over there."

"Those plastic ones with stripes of different colours?"

"Yes."

"They're not school shoes."

"Well, they allow us to wear them."

Mum agreed reluctantly to purchasing the trainers.

"You seem to be in a hurry," she said, as they were exiting the shop. "We'll do a quick trot around the supermarket before going home, if you would help me."

In the store, Mum fired off directions about what to get as she pushed the trolley and picked up the fruit and veg. "Loaf of bread, one-kilo self-rising flour, carton of fruit juice."

Returning with the groceries, Saskia continued the conversation she was having earlier. "I miss Peter being with me." She didn't like to say "at night," as if she was a little kid who needed baby-sitting.

"Peter has at last been in touch with me after he vanished without explanation. He has a job in the metal industry. He was lucky to find work at seventeen."

"Where is he, then?"

"I still don't know. But at least he's earning a living. I was worried about him." She reeled off more items.

Peter doesn't want us to come looking for him, Saskia thought. When she came back again, she threw several packets of groceries one by one into the trolley, as if she were playing basketball.

"Whoa, steady! Something will break open."

"I want everything back to how it was. You living at home. We were happy. You're still married. Dad might come back."

"After twelve years? You can't have everything your own way." Mum wasn't paying attention to it. "Soap powder, two kilos of potatoes, six lamb loin chops."

"I hate your boyfriend!" Saskia cried at her as she marched off to fetch the goods. Quite a few people heard her and turned to stare. *Serve them right.*

Mum became steely and tight-lipped as she caught a punnet of strawberries that flew through the air at her. Then Saskia ran out of steam and withdrew into herself.

Once they were in the car, Mum said, "How dare you embarrass me in the shop!" She was shaking, almost crying.

"What about me? I wish I had a dad."

She grudgingly carried the shopping into the house when they got home. "I've missed half of Star Trek," she whined at Mum who was putting things away in the kitchen. But she knew she was acting like a spoilt kid. Something fell on the floor.

"You wouldn't have if you hadn't had a row with me in the shop!"

Saskia was no longer listening to her. She was absorbed in watching her favourite old program.

After dinner, Saskia and Mum made an uneasy peace.

"I will spend more time with you, Sassy, now you don't have Peter as a companion."

"You remember, Mum, how you said you would take us on a trip to the beach. To see the ocean. You never did."

"Oh dear, it didn't ever fit in with what we were doing. You always enjoyed swimming in our local pool." She spoke absently, sounding non-committal. "I think Mark and I shouldn't stay at each other's houses so much in future. But we like to see each other alternately at his place or mine because it makes us feel equal and secure."

What is that about, Saskia wondered, *I wish she wouldn't call me Sassy. I bet she'll go on treating me as if Peter were around, and I will be alone at night.*

She went to bed, still angry. Mum had said, "I can't believe how bad you've been today." Saskia thought about running away to the coast. She often thought of running away.

In the night, she had one of her dreams about how she rode on the back of a friendly dragon. The dragon spread out its mighty wings, and she climbed up them onto the dragon's back. They flew to the farthest reaches of the universe.

"What is your name?" said the dragon, as they were flying ever upwards above the earth, into a semi-darkness with strange, coloured lights. They were being sucked into a vortex, spiralling down; it was awe-inspiring. It tickled!

"My name is Rider," said Saskia, as her second name was Rider, granny's name. "I can ride forever into space and escape from my enemies. Nobody knows where I am, or how wonderful it is."

Saskia woke up, and said to herself, "I'll call myself Rider. When I run away, I need a new name and identity so that the authorities can't send me back to Mum, or to school. Rider it is."

A couple of nights later, Mum stayed away again all night.

To the Ocean

Saskia stumped into the kitchen for breakfast, opened the fridge door and helped herself to the food Mum always kept in the fridge. She sat down to eat a slice of cold pizza beside the empty chairs. *No one to talk to.*

When she finished eating, she dumped the dirty dishes in the sink. Then and there, she decided to go away on her bike that very day. The summer days were long, and there was no school roll call to catch her out.

She leered at herself mockingly in front of the hall mirror so that her mouth widened and eyes narrowed, and she did a little war dance. She was pleased by her appearance, which was ordinary, with brownish skin, hair, eyes, and a slightly bent nose – she was self-conscious and didn't usually want to stand out. She looked short for her age, having just turned fourteen. She was flat-chested and looked like a boy. *That would be good for security.* She had strong muscles to defend herself.

She put on a cap and picked up her parka in case of bad weather. She pocketed a compass, a penknife, a toothbrush, and tucked a bottle of water and some toilet paper into a small cloth bag. She wouldn't take food because of the food trees that the government had planted all over Australia;

they were growing in the street and in everyone's garden. She thought, *I won't need my mobile phone as I don't want to phone anyone, or get any calls from Mum.*

Saskia slammed the front door behind her and collected her no-puncture bike from the garage. The minute she started to bicycle down the road, she reminded herself, "My name from now on is Rider." The road from their country town led east to the coast. She had never seen the ocean and that was where she wanted to go. If things became intolerable, she would go home.

The cool air of morning rushed past her cheeks, enhancing her sense of excitement as she pedalled fast along the flat road. She noticed that the roads were in a poor state of repair, with many potholes. She chose to ride on the dirt verges, farther away from the huge trucks which suddenly roared past, or cars dodging potholes.

Hearing the sound of a police siren, she jumped off her bike and ducked down behind some bushes. *Suppose they are looking for me?*

"Hey, don't I know you?" a policeman shouted out. But the next second the police had to pull up a speeding car. They booked the driver and left.

Rider, as she was calling herself, became hotter and wearier as the day wore on, and sometimes rested. A small town was a welcome change from being on the road and felt like home. Nothing took away her feeling of freedom.

It was evening when she reached a very small town. She looked for an empty house. Lights were coming on and people were returning home in the ones that were inhabited. After a while, she came across a house on the edge of town that was almost derelict. Leaning her bike against a veranda post, she sat on the veranda. She was hungry and her eyes were drawn to some food trees in the garden. Before it was dark, she ate what she could from the trees: fruit, flowers, nuts, seeds, leaves, and tips of branches.

She was too tired to be afraid. A burglar would probably put his foot through one of the rotten boards on the veranda and sprain his ankle. Bringing all her possessions into the house, Rider fell asleep hugging her bicycle as if it were a suit of armour. There were dogs barking in the neighbourhood, but nothing disturbed her.

The next day, she filled her water bottle at the local shop and headed east again. She hesitated a while, thinking she might ride home, but then kept her bike firmly pointed to the coast. The countryside was greener with more trees and hills. The trees were bigger. Sometimes, she walked up the hills pushing her bike. She felt more alone because she imagined strange things hiding behind the trees. She wished her best friend was with her.

Her best friend had gone to live in another country, Greenland. Most of the ice in Greenland had melted because of global warming. People were flocking there before it closed its borders to permanent settlers, to escape the heat in Australia.

Rider called to mind the special assembly her school held to say goodbye to the kids who were leaving school to go off with their families. All the kids who were splitting up with their friends were crying. When people went away to Greenland, they left behind unoccupied houses.

What's that sound? She stopped cycling and listened. *Is someone moaning?* She walked in the direction of the sound and stopped. A cow, looking at her, stretched out her neck and mooed. The cow was leaning over the fence, pushing it down with effort to try and reach the taller grass on the other side. Rider cropped some of it for her and fed her.

"Hey!" The cow was trying to eat her T-shirt. Rider pulled the cloth out of the cow's mouth, dripping with saliva. She said, "You do slobber a lot." She stroked the cow's soft nose and felt less lonely.

Rider was more fatigued than on the previous day and looked for a house earlier. If she saw no people, cars, or dogs, there would be a good chance the house was vacant, she thought. Again, she found one on the edge of a small town. Inside the house, there was cold tap water to wash in, and worn pants and a T-shirt in a ragbag, so she changed her clothes. Just then, she heard someone coming in and she froze. They would have seen her bike outside.

"Hi." A boy, who was much bigger than Rider, was entering the room. "Do you live here?"

Rider shook her head and almost whispered, "I'm travelling."

"What's your name?"

"Rider."

"I'm Drew. I'm going to Sydney to look for work. What are you doing?"

"I'm going to the coast, to find work too."

"How old are you?"

"Fourteen."

"I'm just sixteen and allowed to leave school. I'm starving." He began to open the cupboard doors. "What can we eat? Dog food!"

"I don't feel very well after eating only from food trees."

"You should have taken some cheese with you," said Drew, and took a chunk of cheese out of his backpack. He cut off a piece and handed it to Rider.

Drew said he would fetch vegetables from the garden and walked out the back door. Rider breathed a sigh of relief; Drew was a kind boy. Rider searched in the cupboards and found some chipped plates and mugs and bent forks they could use. Drew returned with tomatoes and other vegetables, along with the usual food tree supplies, which they ate with tinned dog food.

They were perched on the edge of a lumpy old couch. Drew explained how young people couldn't get paid jobs or much dole. It was because so many people had gone to live in Greenland. They had left what was like a hole in society. People didn't know what the value of money was and mainly traded by barter, which was exchanging things with one another. If you didn't have possessions or skills, you couldn't trade.

"I'll probably get work with someone in exchange for other things I need," he said. He was unsure what it would be like in Sydney.

They brought their bikes into the house for the night. Drew's was solar-powered. They lay down on the carpet to sleep as there were no beds, and slept very soundly.

In the morning, Rider said, "Drew, I've never been to the ocean and I want to go to the coast, not to Sydney."

"Have you got a compass?"

"Yes."

"Then trek southeast to the south coast."

They parted company to go their separate ways. "Good luck!" called Drew from his bike, and he was off.

Rider continued her journey. She realized, once Drew had gone, that he had never recognized that she was a girl. She so much resembled a boy, with her short haircut, shorts, and T-shirt. She had rather a low, husky voice too.

Late in the afternoon, she found a grocery shop in a small town. "Have you got any leftover bread?" she asked the shopkeeper. Drew had told her to do this.

"Yes. I have stale buns, and bruised fruit you can have for free. Now, let me see, there's mouldy cheese, and broken biscuits too."

The woman put the food in a paper bag and handed it to her.

"Gosh, thank you."

"I see your bike out there, with luggage. Are you going far?"

"I'm travelling to my uncle's. He lives at the coast."

Did I tell that complete lie? she thought.

"Take care," said the woman, and waved her goodbye.

Just after Rider spotted her next unoccupied house, calamity struck. She checked the house inside and went outside again. A large, rather fat boy was standing there, surveying her suspiciously.

The Ocean Beckons

The large boy narrowed his eyes and said, "Where do you live?" When Rider didn't reply, the boy said, "You don't belong here." He raised his fist as if to hit her.

Rider didn't wait and started to run. She ran and ran down the street. At the next corner, she looked back. The large boy was in the street in front of the house, staring at her, but he had made no effort to follow. She watched as he took a paper bag out of his pocket, blew it up and burst it with a bang. *Weird.* She turned the corner so that she was out of sight.

She stopped and rested on a street bench. She had some food to eat in her parka, which she was wearing because of light rain earlier. Suddenly, she recalled she had left her bike propped up on the side of the house and it wasn't locked to anything. She jumped up, turned the corner again, and saw the boy had gone. When she got back to the house, the bike was no longer there. *The boy has stolen my bike!*

Rider walked to the other side of the town and found an old hay shed to sleep in, just as darkness fell. It was at the edge of a field with no houses nearby. She didn't have a torch. She lay down with her back against some bales of hay and listened to the loose timbers banging in the wind. A bat flew in under the rickety door. She was sure she could hear the squeaking and scuffling of mice and rats. Something brushed over her face. She shivered. Stiff with fear and cold, she could barely move. She felt sad and lost without her bike. At least burglars wouldn't bother her, for she had nothing to steal now.

Rider thought long and hard that night about returning home. She recalled things that happened to her when she was little; nice or simple things.

Mum let her do the washing up. She pushed a chair over to the sink and climbed on it. Mum ran in warm, soapy water so that the froth piled up and she could blow it into the air.

"Now clean the cups and plates," Mum said. Clatter…clunk…swish…splash!

She helped Mum weed the garden around beds of flowers. Squatting down, she pulled out the weeds and slapped them on the edge of the concrete path the way Mum did, so that the earth fell off their roots.

When they had finished, she said, "Let me pick some flowers, Mum." She put them in a glass jar to decorate the house.

They walked to the grocery shop. She liked to walk along the top of a stonewall in front of the neighbour's house, and on the uneven pine logs at another house where she sometimes lost her balance. She fell against Mum, and Mum righted her. Or she would take a stick and run it along a corrugated metal fence noisily, "rat-tat-tat," as she walked. Or just let her fingers trail on a wire fence and watch it flash past.

Mum tucked her into bed and said, "Good night." She could feel her very close as she hugged and kissed her. For a moment, she clung onto her clothes, and then let go.

One day, her brother came home from school and was too rough with her. The brother tipped her out of her stroller onto the ground. He said, "You are naughty, and I'm going to punish you."

He filled her toy truck with sand and threw the sand in her face. The sand stung her eyes so that she couldn't see clearly and she cried. Mum opened the kitchen door and sent her brother to his room.

As Rider lay on the hard floor of the shed, she had a new appreciation of the comforts of life she would find at home; a soft bed to lie in, someone to talk to, and she had tears in her eyes. The night seemed ages long. But then she fell asleep and dreamed she was holding onto her mother, who pushed her away so she could hurry off with her boyfriend. When Rider woke up in daylight, she remembered she had never seen the ocean, and it would be a shame not to go on if she could.

Still carrying her compass in her pocket, Rider kept walking to the southeast. The land became more wooded. It was hilly, but gradually sloping downhill. She crossed a highway with heavy traffic. She followed it for a while until she came to a sign on a dirt road, which simply said, "To the Coast." She took that road. It was a long walk past tall forest trees with straight, gleaming white trunks. Once, she was shocked when she saw she was face to face with a kangaroo taller than she was. The kangaroo looked like the fat boy as it began to punch the air with its fists. Rider burst out laughing and waved her arms above her head. The kangaroo hopped away swiftly.

Towards evening, Rider thought she could hear the sound of the sea. Soon after, a village came into view. To her joy, she found shops that sold bait and tackle and she knew she was near the sea. She went on walking on a street that pointed east so she could reach the ocean.

The street gave way to a narrow, sandy shoreline where water was continually lapping. But many trees were growing in the water. Rider could hear the waves rolling in and breaking on the shore, but she couldn't really see them. She could see, through the trees, the moon rising; it was large and beautiful like a giant pearl.

In a garden nearby, an old man was taking in his fishing nets for the night. The man called out, "Hello! Are you all right there?"

Rider moved closer and watched him going back and forth to collect the nets. When the man had finished, he beckoned to Rider to come into his house.

As he seemed so friendly, Rider walked cautiously to the front door and said, "I was looking for my uncle, but I couldn't find him."

"You can have some food and stay for the night," said the man, showing her in.

Rider hoped he wouldn't ask awkward questions, as she didn't actually have an uncle. The man said he was a poor fisherman, but he always managed to have a good meal of fish. He cooked the fish straight away and they sat down to eat.

"I've never been to the ocean before," said Rider. "But I can't see it properly because of the trees."

"Those are mangroves. They grow in the saltwater here. The fishing boats are moored at the end of a long jetty that sticks out into the river mouth."

"I wanted to go to a beach."

The man explained that there were some beaches on the coast, but mostly mangroves. Long ago, before the polar ice melted and the oceans rose up and swamped them, sandy beaches were all up and down the coast. Later, there were mangroves and a hotter climate.

The man offered Rider work helping him catch fish, when she was a bigger size.

"It's hard work that doesn't suit everybody," he said. "Some people get seasick."

"Would I be able to buy a bike by catching fish?"

"Yes, a bike, a TV, even a car."

The man went to bed early. He said he didn't have any possessions worth stealing. "There are bad people about who steal children, but not on the coastal path," he warned.

He put Rider to sleep on the couch under blankets, with a lamp on. She felt safe.

In the morning, Rider left before the man was up and took some bread with her. She didn't want to have to explain anything. She decided to follow the edge of the sea south, hoping to find a sandy beach. Seagulls were wheeling and soaring overhead, looking for scraps of food. She couldn't spare any bread to throw to them. She wondered why the fisherman was poor when obviously he could earn whatever he desired. It was a mystery.

Suddenly, an ugly old man appeared out of the bushes and started throwing little stones at her. He laughed.

"Stop that! It's not a nice thing to do to other people."
She began to run. When she looked back, the man had
disappeared.

Rider walked and walked that day along the coast road,
but there were mangroves all the way, their twisted aerial
roots writhing like snakes in the wind and tide. Sometimes,
she glimpsed the open sea when the trees thinned out a little.
Sometimes the ground was sandy; at other times it was
squishy mud that sucked her shoes.

Then, she remembered the fisherman talking about
jetties that projected out into the sea. There was one such
jetty near his house! She had completely forgotten the jetty
because of trying to leave hastily in the morning. So, she
strode on, and at last, she found another one. She clattered
along the loose wooden boards, with mangroves each side,
until she broke free of the trees.

It was low tide on the mudflats. A few boats, bobbing
about, were tied to what was a small jetty. But Rider was
not disappointed because out in front of her was the ocean.
Some headlands hugged the bay nearer the shore. The sea
heaved and fell in continual motion so that the sunshine
sparkled on its surfaces. At some distance, Rider could
discern the white foam of breakers. She tried to make out
the horizon, but there was only a hazy blue between the sky
and the sea. She wondered if fish were swimming about,
and peered down into the water. Not one. But a crab was
scrabbling around in the mud!

When Rider reached another coastal town late in the
day, a corner shop was open where she could ask for
leftover food.

"What is this town?" she said.

"Woogoo," said the shopkeeper. "It means 'exchange' in an aboriginal language. Where do you want to go?"

"I'd like to climb a hill to see a view of the ocean."

"The road from here goes straight up a hill," said the woman, pointing towards the inland.

Rider set off at once in that direction, passing houses in the town and crossing the main road. Next, she was walking on a dirt road running gently uphill past farms and patches of bushland.

She stopped eventually when the road ended at another road that cut across it to form a T-junction. She was at a high point, and turned to look back down the road she had ascended. There was a sweeping view of the town below and, beyond that, the ocean. Now, she could see a wide expanse of water with tiny white crests of foam and, because the weather had cleared, the faint line of the horizon. There were ships out at sea, yachts with sails near the shore, and boats anchored at jetties. Rider was excited. *One day I will find a sandy beach*, she thought, *where I can surf the waves.*

Jeff

After Rider had finished looking at the view of the ocean, she crossed the road. She heard the sounds of someone working in their backyard. She could see a house on what appeared to be a large bush block. Parting some bushes at the front of the block, she watched an older man saw up timber into shorter lengths to make a top for an outdoor table. He was bald and had good muscles like a person used to doing physical work. If the man was alone, Rider thought she would talk to him later when it was getting dark, just as she had to the fisherman. The man might give her a meal and bed her down for the night.

Rider was exhausted. She leaned against the bushes, which made a rustling noise. Immediately, two dogs who had been lying in the shadows ran towards her, barking.

The man called to the dogs, "What is it?" and they stopped short of jumping up at Rider, but wagged their tails furiously, and yelped. The man was walking over, saying, "Good dog, good dog." He came closer and Rider said, "I like dogs."

"Are you hungry?" asked the man of the dishevelled boy he saw, not fully grown, who was a stranger to him. There were many waifs these days.

"Come inside and I'll get you something to eat."

He helped Rider over the fence and turned to walk back to the house. Rider was glad to follow with the two friendly dogs.

Seated at the kitchen table, they had some milk and delicious, crunchy algae-and-insect biscuits. The man said, "I am called Jeff. What is your name?"

"My name's Rider."

"You look as if you have come a long way."

"I was travelling to the ocean. I've never seen it before."

"Have you got a home somewhere?"

Rider explained she had left home to look for work. There were few jobs in her small country town. "I'm nearly fifteen and can leave school," she said. *He won't guess I've only just turned fourteen.*

"So, you are seeking an apprenticeship or training for a job?"

"Yes."

Rider told him more about why she ran away from home and her journey. She slept in unoccupied houses; she could get free food and old clothes. She was puzzled as to why the fisherman she stayed with was poor when he said Rider could earn anything by working as a fisherman.

Jeff said, "Firstly, the fisherman is only allowed to catch a certain amount of fish, and there are not as many fish to catch these days.

"When he was young, people had to work most of their lives to pay off a house. It was the main challenge in life. But now there are many houses vacated by those who migrated to the cooler climate of Greenland that people can live in for free because the houses are proving difficult to sell. Now, the challenge is to survive in a hot and depleted environment."

Rider felt her head nodding to one side and then coming back up with a jerk. After Jeff said he must go outside to do some chores, she became wide awake again. They walked to a paddock nearby where Jeff kept a grove of food trees fenced separately from his animals so that they wouldn't damage it. The trees were natives crossed with cactuses, he said. Jeff sawed off some branches while Rider threw them over a fence for his cow and sheep to eat.

"There's not much grass for them these days because of the hot, dry climate," Jeff explained. They carried back to the house some of the food tree that was nice for humans and collected eggs that the chickens had laid.

Rider saw skins of animals stretched out on the wire fence to dry in the sun. They were mainly rabbit skins, but there was one that could have been a kangaroo and another that looked like a crocodile. Jeff said he was going to make things with the skins. He had a struggle to overpower the crocodile and male kangaroo as he was not allowed to use a gun on a five-acre block. His clever mongrel dogs helped him. The crocodile just turned up in his waterhole one day.

It was beginning to get dark and Jeff set about preparing a meal before nightfall. Whether he was working in the kitchen or out on the back porch, he often mumbled to himself or whistled a few notes of a song. Rider played with the two dogs on the floor. She was sitting on a sheepskin rug with a soft, deep pile.

"We're having rabbit for our dinner," said Jeff.

While they were eating, Jeff said he was a retired person living on his own.

"Do you ever feel lonely?"

"Well, there's nothing I can do about it. Surely you don't feel lonely at home with your family."

"Mmm." Rider didn't feel like explaining anything. "I'm enjoying the rabbit."

After dinner, Jeff brought some blankets for Rider to sleep under on the sofa, where she would feel happier in the night near the dogs, he said. Rider had a warm shower in the bathroom and was amazed at how much dirt came off her body. She couldn't recollect when she last had a shower.

Jeff said, "Please stick around and don't rush away. We can talk more about what you would like to do in the future, and I haven't shown you the rest of my place yet. I have skills to pass on and friends who could be helpful to you."

In the morning, after a hearty breakfast, Rider went with Jeff to the spare room, where there were old clothes she could wear that Jeff's family had discarded. The clothes were too big, with shorts down to her knees and a sloppy T-shirt, but she regarded them as being in fashion. For footwear, she still had the sturdy trainers Mum had bought her, a bit grubby and worse for wear.

Then they were off to milk the cow. Opening the gate to the paddock, Jeff called the horned cow, whose name was Yak, "Yak, Yak, Yak, Yakety-Yak!" and she came through the gateway and followed Jeff and Rider to her milking stall in the shed.

"Watch out for the sheep," said Jeff. "Shut the gate, or she will slip out when your back is turned." The sheep, Ivana the Terrible, looked terrible after being shorn and was terribly hard to catch.

A wooden bar held the cow's head in position so she could eat some food in the manger while they milked her by hand into a pail. Jeff tied one of her back legs so that she couldn't "Kick the bucket," he joked. Rider sat on a stool, and Jeff showed her how to squeeze and pull gently on the cow's teats in order to squirt milk into the bucket. The milk was warm and frothy. After milking, they walked the cow back to her paddock.

Over at the back fence, a horse's head appeared and Jeff said it was his horse, Caesar, which he was grazing on an unoccupied bush block.

"I've never ridden a horse," said Rider.

Jeff got the saddle and bridle and put them on the horse.

"Put your left foot in the stirrup, heave yourself up, and raise your right leg over to the other side of the horse."

He helped push Rider up onto the saddle. He showed her how to hold the reins.

Jeff led the horse around the paddock at first, walking. Then he started running to make the horse trot. Once he had done a few rounds of the paddock with the horse trotting, and trying to tell Rider how to rise up and down in the stirrups to the trot, he was too puffed out to continue.

Jeff took Rider to see a little creek he had that was more like a dark, boggy hole. It was surrounded by native plants that grew there naturally. When it rained, the hollow filled with water and the frogs would croak. When the wind was blowing, the casuarinas made a whirring and shushing sound. Birds loved this spot.

"You might come across anything here."

He sometimes found echidnas, protected animals, sitting in the muddy shallows cooling their stomachs.

Returning to the house, Jeff drew Rider's attention to the brass nameplate *Endeavour* screwed onto the outside wall.

"The house was named after Captain Cook's ship. He discovered Australia in the *Endeavour* for the British, you know. When the people who built this house looked out at the magnificent view of the ocean from the front of it, they felt they were on a ship seeing something for the first time."

"I know how that feels, from when I saw the ocean for the first time."

In the afternoon they took a respite from the summer's heat inside the house. Jeff had a study lined with books on all the walls. Some of them were very old and were collected and passed on in his family. They were from a time before computers.

"You can read these books, and use the computer too," said Jeff. He told Rider that he once worked in an agricultural business, advising farmers what to plant and stock. He had taught himself carpentry and many skills needed in repairing a house. A young person would be able to find work in that field.

"Won't your mother be worried about you?" Jeff asked suddenly. Rider cast down her eyes. "You could write her a note to say you are okay."

"When I'm older, I'll go and see her again," said Rider, with a pained expression on her face.

Jeff told Rider how his family went to live in Greenland: his son with his wife and their two children, his sister and daughter. Jeff's wife died before all this occurred. So, he was the only member of his family still in Australia. He missed his grandchildren in particular. He would wake up in the middle of the night and wonder how his grandchildren were and what they looked like now, and tears would form in his eyes and roll down his cheeks. It would be a long way to go to the opposite side of the world to see them in Greenland. The families were living in small flats and there was a lack of other accommodation.

"But I'll make a trip there some time, and take a tent and sleeping bag. I imagine they have camping grounds in Greenland."

Rider felt very touched by Jeff's story. She wasn't hard-hearted, but she couldn't think what to say. A dog started barking.

"That's Barker," said Jeff. "I forgot to feed the dogs."

"Is his name really Barker?" said Rider, glad to change the subject. "It's not very original."

Jeff was on the move, with Rider behind him. "Dog's names need to be easy to call out. The other one is Pogo."

Going through the kitchen, Jeff thrust a packet of dog food into Rider's hands: "You feed them. I have to get something."

Jeff joined Rider outside a few minutes later, holding a pogo stick. It had pedals mounted on springs, and you could jump up and down on it balanced on the metal rod.

"Have a go," said Jeff, after giving a demonstration.

Rider jumped up and down, banging the end of the rod on the ground and trying not to lose her balance. Barker barked all the time she did it, and Pogo jumped up and down on all fours. Rider laughed and laughed till tears came out of her eyes. Every time she lost her balance and came off the stick, the dogs stopped barking and jumping. The instant she started jumping again they started barking and jumping.

After dinner, Jeff made up a bed for Rider in the spare room. He said Rider could sleep on the sofa near the dogs at any point she wanted to. He put the pogo stick away in his tool shed and showed Rider some tools she might like to use. Rider helped with the washing up and learned how to load the dishwasher. Jeff set the robot vacuum cleaner on go.

"Everything runs on solar power these days," he said. "Cars, ships, planes, factories. It turns sea and wastewater into freshwater. It's very cheap and makes life easy for people, like the food trees."

Jeff switched on the TV and said Rider was welcome to watch it. It mostly had repeat programs, occasional news, and some people from the local community talking.

"They're not making new programs," said Jeff, and soon switched the TV off.

Out of the blue, Rider said: "Rider isn't my real name. I made it up so the authorities couldn't send me back to my mother, and to school."

"Never mind," said Jeff, who was feeling awkward about his position. If Rider did not wish to go home, Jeff at least wanted to stop her travelling from one place to another and falling into unscrupulous hands. He pointed out to her that she could do correspondence school by studying at home and sending in her assignments. When she was fifteen, she would be able to attend a training college.

"You are always free to go, Rider, and you are brave and resourceful, but I hope you don't go just yet – there are dangers. Rumour has it that children are being kidnapped and taken to Sydney to work in the drugs trade!"

All this time, he doesn't know I'm a girl, thought Rider. She paid no attention to Jeff's talk of kidnappers.

The windows began to rattle. Jeff said the weather was brewing up for a storm. They both went out to take in the animal skins that were stretched on the fence. They were thoroughly dry.

In the night, there was a strong wind, moaning and wuthering, "Woo, woo." It buffeted the roof, making it shake and thump. Rider woke up and listened to it, but she felt so comfortable in her bed that she couldn't be bothered to get up and sleep on the sofa near the dogs. *I'll go if it gets worse*, she thought. But the next minute she fell back to sleep.

Barter

When Rider woke up, she felt warm and safe in the bed at Jeff's house.

"The cyclone season is coming soon," said Jeff. Rider and Jeff were looking at damage from the threatening wind in the night. The door of the shed was loose. In the garden, vegetables like corn and capsicum that were growing around the house were knocked about. The tomato plants had partly fallen from their stakes and needed tying up again.

"We'll go shopping today," Jeff said. "I have homemade cheese to take in and exchange for fish at the market."

Jeff put on his hat to protect his bald head from the sun, and they went in the car down the hill to Woogoo. The town was set back from the coastal mangroves on a gently rising slope, with playing fields on the flat ground lower down. There was an outdoor market with stalls on the edge of town. Jeff said it was running nearly every day because it was the easiest way to shop with the barter system people used nowadays. Fish was the main produce.

"Many people just angle with a fishing rod out on the long jetty and pull in the fish they want for free, but they don't always get any," said Jeff. "We'll do it sometime."

Jeff took his matured cheese to one of the stalls and swapped it for a large fish. He wanted a loaf of bread, so he exchanged some of his tomatoes for it.

Jeff was continually saying "Hello," and talking to people he knew. If they asked about Rider, Jeff said she was doing odd jobs.

As they were passing the fish market, a man called out to Rider,

"Did you find your uncle?"

"Yes."

After they moved away, she explained to Jeff that it was the fisherman from the neighbouring village she had stayed with, and how she said she was looking for an uncle she didn't have.

"I am happy to be your uncle," said Jeff.

Rider decided to wander around the shops on her own. She was hoping to find a bike shop. Ambling about scrutinizing the wares in shop windows, she noticed a boy who seemed to be trailing her. He looked even more ordinary than she did! There were few people in the street, as they had gone to the market. Any moment the boy thought Rider was watching him, he directed his gaze at a shop window. Clearly, the boy didn't want to talk to her. Maybe he had a mind to steal something. When she walked up closer to him, he turned and glared at her without saying anything.

On the way home, Jeff stopped near a patch of old native rainforest. They walked quite a distance through the winding, clinging, stinging vines and straggly creepers, to a small spring Jeff knew about where he could fill his water bottle.

"I found this spring once, in case I ever needed some water."

"There's water everywhere in the taps!"

"When there isn't much natural freshwater, you should know where to find it. It's part of my bush knowledge."

"I don't think I'll come along this path again. It's too creepy. I might meet a ghost or a deranged person."

"There is a deranged man in Woogoo who frightens children."

"I think I've already met him. He threw stones at me."

Jeff wanted to get home for lunch, because he had made an appointment for early in the afternoon to see his friend and near neighbour, Venetia. He was going to carry out repairs to her shed and fences. Rider was very surprised when he harnessed the horse, Caesar, to an old cart. Tossing the carpentry tools and wood materials into the cart, the two of them jumped in, shook the reins, and called "Giddy-up" and "Gee-up" to the horse. They trotted away, bumping and laughing along the rutted dirt road.

"I will leave Caesar outside Venetia's place to graze the frowsy grass that is growing on the edges of the road," Jeff said. "He'll be attached to the cart and won't stray far."

Venetia was waiting for them in her front garden. She wore a brightly coloured tie-dyed dress. She seemed pleased to meet Rider.

"I hear you are being a great help to Jeff."

She pointed out what she needed to be done, and Jeff and Rider got to work. Rider held down pieces of wood while Jeff measured, saw, and hammered. He said that much of the "wood" he used was fabricated waste material pressed into sheets. Some fences needed straightening up and strengthening and Jeff had tools for doing that too, while Rider gripped and steadied posts in place.

When they had finished the woodwork, Venetia wanted a chicken killed, and Rider was to come inside while Jeff did the job. Venetia introduced Rider to a ten-year-old girl, Katie, from next-door who was helping to roll up balls of wool. There were skeins of wool hanging from a hook on the wall. Katie had straight dark hair like Venetia, so she could almost have been her daughter. Venetia said, "I have two sheep which supply me with milk and wool."

She sat down at her spinning wheel and spun some wool into yarn, so Rider and Katie could see how the pieces of wool were joined and made thinner. "I will use the yarn for knitting, but I'm learning to weave blankets with it, too."

She said she wove mats just with pieces of wool. Jeff had one of them in his house.

Venetia had made a lovely sponge cake with strawberries and cream on it, topped with whirls of chocolate. Jeff returned, and they had cups of tea and ate all the cake between them.

"I'd like to have long woollen socks to wear with my working boots," said Jeff. "Would you teach me how to knit them with your yarn?"

Venetia said she would knit them for him. "You can still buy these things in the shops, Jeff," she said. Laughing, she turned to Rider, "Jeff thinks we will have to go back to a past when people made their own clothes, grew all their food, and used horses for transport."

"He made a sundial in case we don't have clocks anymore."

But Jeff said a bit grumpily that he couldn't get socks that were big enough. Otherwise, he was managing with his thin old clothes and blankets, which was all he needed in a hot climate. In the future, he might learn to make boots and belts from his leather skins.

Venetia took Rider to see the garden pots she made from clay she dug up on her own land. She grew herbs and vegetables in them and also sold them. Placing a lump of clay on her potter's wheel, she turned the wheel fast and fashioned with her hands, like magic, a perfect pot. She told Rider to try it. The clay wobbled as the wheel rotated, but she guided Rider's hands with hers and together, they made a wavy-edged vase.

"I'll fire that vase for you later," she said. "Rider, you are welcome to come and talk with me about any problems you have, things to do with your family, changes in your body, and so on. I am here, ready to listen, and trying to be helpful."

Rider nodded.

It was time to go home. They found Caesar the horse had eaten a patch of grass so that it appeared to be mown. He had also deposited from his other end, a pongy mound of manure for the garden.

Katie was delighted to have a ride in the cart. They would drop her off at her house on the way. As they set off, she was saying, "Er, er, er," listening to her voice go up and down every time the cart jerked on the rough track and then bursting into giggles. In answer to questioning, she said she had plenty of friends her own age at school, but none nearby. Her mother was her only company at home.

When Jeff and Rider arrived at Jeff's place, the branches of food trees blown down in the wind the night before had to be thrown over the fence for the animals to eat.

Jeff and Rider were dirty from head to toe. Just for fun, Jeff thought he would demonstrate the bush shower on a rope pulley he had rigged up once in the backyard. It was a large tin that could be filled with water and had little holes punched in the base. You opened a cover, and water came out of the holes.

Rider decided to take a shower with her clothes on. *Brrr. Cold!* The dogs kept coming up to her and licking the water as it was dripping off. After having the shower, she ran about with the dogs, shouting and throwing a ball and stick for them to fetch. She was worn out before the dogs were, because of her energetic activities that day. By then, her clothes were almost dry again.

Jeff handed her a pair of old, clean pyjamas to wear. He said,

"If you agree to it, I'm going to put the dogs outside tonight, which is what I normally do. You might have seen their kennels. They guard the house, catch and eat rats, and stop rabbits from eating the vegetables. Barker woofs softly sometimes, but you get used to it. If a stranger came, they would bark loudly."

While having their dinner of fish, Rider said she would like to meet others of her age to play games. She used to play football at school and cricket sometimes with her brother. Jeff said there would be children playing sports in

Woogoo tomorrow, Saturday. He would phone some friends and find out where the teams were playing.

"I wish you would write a letter to your mother to say you're all right. Imagine how she feels, not knowing where you are. She must feel worried. Or miss you and be sad."

"But I don't want her to know where I am. I don't want to be sent back to her. The letter would be stamped Woogoo Post Office."

"Then we'll post it from somewhere else."

So, Rider wrote this letter to her mother:

Dear Mum, I am well and safe. I am staying with a fairly old man and doing work for him. I can do correspondence school. Don't worry about me. Love from Saskia.

Jeff drove Rider to the village where she had lodged with the fisherman and she posted the letter there, in her pyjamas. She did not show Jeff the name, Lilian Smith, and the address on the envelope. She thought of telling Jeff she was a girl but didn't feel like it yet. It wasn't the right moment. *If he notices my washing on the clothesline, I guess he wouldn't realize my underpants are hand-me-downs from my brother.*

When Saskia's mum, Lilian, came home and found that Saskia was absent and her bike was gone, she thought at first that she might be out with school friends. She cursed her for leaving her mobile phone behind. She waited till later in the day to phone people she knew, but they hadn't seen anything of Saskia. In the evening, she walked around looking for her and called in to the police station to say that she couldn't find her. Only one policeman was on duty. He said Saskia might be staying with friends and to come back in the morning. She could hardly sleep, expecting her to turn up any time of the night. When Saskia still hadn't appeared, she returned to the police station as soon as it opened.

The police said they would search for her and drive around the roads. That's what she did too, day after day until the letter arrived. Every night, she lay awake wondering what had happened to Saskia, where she had gone and why, worrying whether she had been the victim of an accident or crime. Had she been kidnapped, raped, or murdered? When she received the letter, she felt relieved but couldn't be sure that Saskia was really all right. She felt frustrated that she couldn't get in touch with her.

The police put Saskia on their list of missing children and promised they would make every effort to find her. It would take time. Sometimes these children turned up of their own accord.

"Keep in contact with us with any new information, but don't worry yourself about her," said the policeman. "She sounds like a very independent girl."

Cricket and Work

On Saturday, Rider walked down the long hill to Woogoo with the view of the ocean, to watch the sports matches on the playing fields. She took with her a map, a cheese sandwich, and Jeff's name, address, and phone number written in a note.

If people asked her about herself, she could use Jeff's surname, which was Milgate, and say she was Jeff's nephew. (Jeff didn't have nephews and nieces. He had said, "I hereby adopt you as my nephew." He gave Rider his old boy scout badge with *Jeffrey Milgate* inscribed on it.) Or Rider could say she worked for Jeff in return for board. Jeff was known and respected in the community.

When she reached the sports ground, Rider watched a football match for a while.

"They are school teams," a parent standing on the sidelines told her. Rider didn't want to join those because the authorities might find out who she was.

Next, she closely observed a game of basketball but thought she was too short to play it. She saw boys and girls playing tennis, but then she thought she was too young to mix with their older crowd. Finally, she arrived at the

Cricket Club, and they had children of all ages playing there. She asked one of the adults if she could join the club.

"Of course, you can," the man said and pointed to where she could. She signed up, writing *Rider Milgate*. She was directed to the nets to practice bowling and batting, and someone in charge saw that she had the right equipment. A queue of kids was waiting to practice and they said a friendly "Hello." The coach put Rider in to bat and then to bowl, and said she could join a team who were starting a game after lunch. Many had brought their own food and they sat together on the edge of the playing field, eating it.

While Rider was waiting to bat, she talked with the other players. Some of them were at school and others attended the technical college. A few had dropped out, like Rider.

A boy next to her said, "My name's Axel." He had gingery hair, fair skin and freckles, and splodges of zinc cream over his face to prevent sunburn, which looked like war paint. *Right on*, Rider thought. *Cool.*

"What's your name?" Axel said.

"Rider."

"Do you live in Woogoo?"

"Yes, up on the hill with my uncle."

"Do you go to high school?" said Axel, knowing he had never seen Rider there.

"No."

"I stopped going to high school."

"Why?"

Axel stared down at the dirt, where he was drawing with a stick. He said, "Aw, I didn't like it," in a subdued voice, as if he didn't want to talk any more.

Keeping an eye on how the game was going, Rider felt in her pockets for anything interesting. She came up with her compass and a piece of string. She nudged Axel and started explaining how the compass worked. Axel already knew, "From Scouts," he said. But he took the string and showed Rider how to tie a reef knot.

"It won't come undone unless you untie it."

At that moment, their conversation ended as someone was caught out and it was Rider's turn to bat.

Late in the day, Rider was walking up to Jeff's place when she became aware of a boy following a short distance behind her. Every time Rider turned around to look at him, the boy stopped and seemed to peer at something on the side of the road. Rider had a feeling that the boy, who was bigger than she was, was following her. She thought it was the boy she had seen on market day. When Rider halted at the top of the hill to take in the view, the boy had disappeared.

Rider found Jeff resting in the library, reading books. He had worked in the garden and killed a chicken for Sunday dinner. Rider told him about the game of cricket, and Axel, and how their team won, but not about the boy who trailed her up the hill. After all, the boy might just have been walking home.

Rider said she would like to work for Jeff, but she didn't know what she could do.

"Children under fifteen are not allowed to work by law," replied Jeff. "But you can contribute to your board. Now, I have discovered how you can do correspondence school."

Rider hardly heard Jeff talking about correspondence school. She was thinking of working to get a solar-powered bike. At this moment, she realized she would have to wait until she was fifteen to work before she could buy the bike.

In the morning, Jeff said that Rider could accompany him around the garden to see what work she could do. They took most of the food scraps to the chickens, even crushed eggshells. They tossed the rest of the rubbish on the compost heap.

Jeff had been weeding and putting manure and mulch around the potatoes and carrots, which were developing underground. He plucked a carrot out of the ground by its leaves, waved it in the air and said *"Voilà!"* like someone performing a magic trick. He was growing an enormous zucchini protected from rabbits in one of Venetia's pots.

"I will weed around the vegetables," said Rider.

Jeff had tried to grow fruit trees without chemical sprays but they had mostly died of diseases or were attacked by insects. Some apricots were flourishing and they picked the ripe fruit.

The water tank collected water from the roof whenever it rained, which wasn't often. The spare water, and waste from the septic tank, went through pipes to the plants and helped them grow.

"It's not possible nowadays to grow much grain like wheat for bread because the climate is so hot and dry," Jeff said. "The bread we buy is labelled 'plant material,' whatever it is. Paper is made of 'waste' plant material!"

They went to look at the traps. These were conical cylinders of fine mesh blocked at the narrow end, with glue in them. They were placed on the ground at various spots. They could trap snakes, rabbits, and mice. There was nothing today.

"You're allowed to catch and kill snakes, cats, rabbits, foxes, crocodiles, and male kangaroos on your own land for food," said Jeff. "Snakes used to be protected, but farmers often killed them. Cats are supposed to be prohibited by law. Female kangaroos are saved because they have babies. Rabbits and foxes are pests and can be killed anywhere. I wish I could catch the fox hiding on the unoccupied block at the back, but it does keep the rabbits down and hasn't got into the chicken pen yet."

"Could the fox hurt me?"

"No, they slink away from humans and dogs."

"I will inspect the traps every day and tell you what there is," said Rider.

"Mind the venomous snakes and the bees!" said Jeff and pointed to the beehives in box houses he had for bush bees. "I don't mean to frighten you about snakes. They are rarely caught in the traps. Snakes live underground most of the time. Come and tell me if you find one. If you ever see a snake hole in the ground, jam a stone in it to block the hole."

After this excursion, Rider truly appreciated her lunch of corn on the cob, carrot sticks, honey on bread made without grains, apricots, and milk. She had an idea.

"I will milk the cow every day," she volunteered.

"If you milk the cow that is a really adult and responsible thing to do. A cow can't be left unmilked. You can milk the cow once a day and I'll milk it the other time."

"Done!" said Rider, catching Jeff's habit of exclaiming things.

On Monday, Jeff received a business letter. A trader in Sydney was offering to buy his crocodile and kangaroo skins for a good sum. He was actually paying cash for them. Jeff thought he would accept the offer.

"I can put the money in my savings account in the government-owned bank, which is the only bank now operating in Australia. I have to pay the government land and water rates on my property, and I have an agreement for them to take the fees out of my bank account. The payment from the trader will top up my account, as it is constantly shrinking."

Rider remembered how she used to raid her piggy bank. "What if you ran out of money and couldn't pay the rates?"

"I don't think anyone knows. It's part of the hole in society caused by the large numbers of people going to Greenland. The government isn't paying much pension. But at least the environment should profit from the absence of people. Then, we all would too."

How would we profit? wondered Rider.

Gav and Other Matters

As the days passed, Rider settled into doing correspondence school. She usually completed it in half a day. In the afternoons, she often helped Jeff because she liked it and always milked the cow in the late afternoon. She sometimes read in Jeff's library because the books were interesting. Every Saturday, she walked down to the sports field in Woogoo to play cricket. She made friends with Axel.

The second time Rider was coming back from the sports field, she saw the strange boy following her again. She picked a stick up off the ground casually to use if he threatened her, and turned to face him before he reached where he disappeared last time. Then, she walked back down the hill towards the boy, who stood his ground.

"Do you live around here?" Rider enquired.

"I have friends. What's your name?"

"Rider."

"I never heard that name."

Rider shrugged her shoulders. "Who are you?"

"They call me Gav."

Rider started to turn away.

"You don't belong here," Gav continued, raising his voice.

"What, in Woogoo?"

"Yes."

Rider surprised herself by saying, "I belong to Australia."

"What, the whole of Australia?"

"Yes."

As Gav only stood there with his mouth open, Rider kept on walking up the hill.

Rider next crossed paths with Gav on the sports field one Saturday. Gav asked her if she went to the high school.

"No, do you?"

"No, I go to the technical college."

"I'm going there later this year."

Gav looked around to see whether anyone was within earshot. Then he said, "You're thin and scrawny like a chicken, and the boys at Tech would pound you to mincemeat in a few seconds."

Rider stared back at him very hard. Her mind was in turmoil. She wanted to say she was strong but decided to be silent. She remembered how she used to fight with her brother, but that was play-fighting. So, she turned her back on Gav and walked away. But she was still churned up inside about it. She asked the children at cricket if they knew Gav.

"Yes, he is a bully," a boy said.

"Don't have anything to do with him," said a girl.

Rider told Jeff about Gav and what he'd said.

"Do you think Gav would hurt you physically?" asked Jeff.

"I don't know. I don't like the nasty remarks he made."

"They're obviously untrue. I think Gav is probably a coward when it actually comes to fighting."

Rider was not so sure. "He's bigger than I am. I think I'd like to learn how to defend myself. I'd feel better."

Rider found out where children could learn martial arts and took herself off to the classes. They were free, being run by community volunteers. The children were taught a variety of unarmed combat moves, mostly from Judo, which used sparring or grappling. They could trap their opponent on the ground or in a standing arm lock. They were taught not to hurt their opponent but only to force them to submit. There were rules to adhere to.

Rider loved the classes. She could fraternize with other children in the clubhouse (an old church hall). She particularly liked the fact that girls were learning martial arts. She liked the girls; they didn't giggle as much as Katie but were older and took life more seriously. It was important for girls to defend themselves.

After doing some martial arts classes, Rider told Jeff she felt more able to cope with Gav, including his mean and nasty words. Jeff said they probably hadn't heard the last of Gav.

Rider walked round to Venetia's place to collect the pottery vase that Venetia was going to fire for her. Katie was visiting and Rider told her about the girls doing martial arts.

"I'll do it next year when I go to high school," said Katie. "It is a good idea."

Rider discussed Gav and the martial arts classes with Axel. Axel said, "I gave up high school because a boy picked on me." He would think about joining the classes.

"How did he pick on you?"

"He used to snatch the biro out of my hand. He bumped into me so that I dropped my books. He called me names that meant I was stupid. But I'm not."

Axel invited Rider to a sleepover at his home. Axel, who was nearly fourteen, had started correspondence school also. He wanted Rider to come over to discuss the correspondence courses and play some board games. Rider discovered that Axel had many enjoyable games she had never played like Monopoly, Go, backgammon, Chinese checkers, and Scrabble. Rider was given few games or toys when she was little.

Axel's mother asked Rider if she was staying with her uncle for a holiday.

"No, it's because my mother isn't well, but she has a friend who comes in to help."

She became flustered and awkward as she said it since it wasn't true. She then thought the others could read guilt all over her face. Axel's mother didn't ask further questions.

When Rider returned to Jeff's house, she found Jeff had been looking for games in his collections that they could play together. He turned up a chessboard, complete with pieces, and taught Rider chess. He also had a gambling game for adults, roulette. They played roulette, which was more relaxing, with pretend money.

Rider said, "I like having a man in my life," and was surprised because it was true; her father had mostly been absent, and she just said it without thinking. That had happened to her a lot lately.

"I was lucky to find you, Jeff."

"This is your home for as long as you would like."

Rider fidgeted.

"Jeff, I haven't told you the truth about me. Rider isn't my real name."

I'm always lying so much.

"Well, so you said before. It is a rather unusual name. And remember about your secretly posting a letter to your mother? I don't know your surname or address either."

"No. You see, I'm really a girl." Rider blushed and looked away from Jeff. "I always look like a boy so people think I am a boy."

"Goodness me! I'd never have guessed it. But I'm not cross with you."

"It won't make any difference. I can still do all the work you gave me to do, just like a boy."

"Why don't you like your real name? What is it?"

"My real name is Saskia," said Rider, burying her face in her hands. "Eeerrr. But when I decided to run away, I thought Rider, my second name, would be better to hide my identity. I didn't realize, then, that people would think I was a boy. But it was convenient because it protected me from how they might treat me as a lone girl."

"You are a courageous person, Rider," said Jeff.

The next time Rider saw Axel, she knew she had to tell him the truth about her gender and not continue to deceive him. She said she was a girl who just looked like a boy, and now, he probably wouldn't like her any more. Axel was amazed. But he was still her friend, he said.

It was ironic that a full-blown cyclone came one night, just after Jeff offered Rider his house as her home for as long as she liked. The cyclone shook the house to its foundations. It sounded like an express train or a plane in close range. Rider cowered under the bed, expecting something to fall down any minute. She understood now the fears Jeff felt in these cyclones.

She drifted back to sleep and dreamed that she was in a house that was burning down. She screamed for help and her father came and picked her up and carried her to safety.

Someone was calling, "Are you all right?" It was Jeff standing beside her bed.

"Yes."

"I've let the dogs inside."

The roof seemed to be lifting up and slamming down. Bang! Bang! Bang! They were both awake for hours, on tenterhooks.

In the morning, Jeff said it was a typical cyclone. The old brick and stone house would be hard to knock over. The windows were small with colonial panes, so it would be difficult to break them. He was always working at reinforcing the roof to keep it on.

They went outside later to survey the damage and were pleased it had rained. Most of the taller growing vegetables were flattened, but not necessarily dead. Rider observed how everything was placed close to, or leaning against the house: the shed, the dog kennels, the chicken house. Venetia's capacious pots filled with earth and plants were positioned to stabilize things, and couldn't be budged. Jeff had put wire across the metal roof at intervals, which went on down the walls to where heavy stones pinned it to the ground.

"Do you think some roofs might have blown off in Woogoo?" Rider asked.

"It's quite possible, but we bear the brunt of the storm because we are higher up, and they are more protected."

Over at the grove of food trees, more branches had fallen than usual which they fed to the animals or took home. Jeff said food trees were pretty resistant to wind, storm, fire, drought, salt in the soil, insects, and diseases. They grew quickly, regenerated easily, and supported one another.

"Unless we have a catastrophe," said Jeff, "everything will remain much the same."

As it turned out, he would be proved wrong.

Sandy Beach

Rider had always wanted to go to a beach and surf the waves. Her wish came true one weekend early in autumn. Jeff found out where there was a sandy beach, farther down the south coast. They would take a picnic lunch for a day trip. Rider invited Axel to come too. There was a spare seat, so Jeff said he would like to ask Katie, as she had asked Rider to her party – Jeff had told Katie and Venetia that Rider was a girl.

Rider made a disagreeable face and said, "I suppose so."

She had been a guest at Katie's eleventh birthday when she invited mostly girls from her school and not many boys. The girls wore party frocks and some even had makeup. Rider went dressed in the white cricket pants Jeff had found in his cupboards, and a white T-shirt. It didn't occur to either of them to buy a dress, as Rider didn't like them. She hoped the girls wouldn't take any notice of her. But they giggled.

Katie said she would like to come to the beach so that she could collect shells to make into jewellery, and seaweed to take home to eat. Katie, Axel, and Rider had all learned to swim in primary school, they assured Jeff, including rescue and resuscitation. They came dressed in their swimmers, with T-shirts for sun protection. Rider wore a one-piece swimsuit from Jeff's collection of old clothes. Katie sat in the front of the car with Jeff, while the other two chatted in the back with eager anticipation of surfing.

The coast road they drove down was forested at first, occasionally with burnt-out areas from a bushfire. Jeff said the fires were caused by lightning strikes. The trees began to clear; there were small farms and glimpses of the sea. At last, they took the turnoff to Sandy Beach and they had arrived.

"Hurray, hurry!" shouted the young ones and sprang out of the car with one accord, "I'll beat you to the sea!"

They ran down the sand to the water, deliberately splashing one another as they waded in. On the beach, there were a few other people, flags to swim between, and it was patrolled by lifesavers. Rider and Axel raced out for the breakers, though Rider had never experienced surf before, leaving Katie to jump and catch waves in the shallows.

Soon, Rider was up to her chest in water, being dumped face first in the sand or rolled over, and then dragged back into the sea by breakers before she could catch them. But she was ecstatic, laughing as she came up gasping for air. After a while, she got the idea of trying to drive for the shore well before the wave broke. She felt envious of the kids who had surfboards.

When they had been out surfing waves for a long time, the shark alarm sounded. Jeff had been paddling in the water with Katie until she went back up to the beach. He was keeping an eye on the other two and saw them starting to swim for the shore with all the surfers. Looking farther out to sea, he spotted the shark's fin. A patrol boat was out there too, but it was difficult to see how near the boat, the shark, and the swimmers were to one another.

Rider and Axel heard the shark alarm and swam towards the beach. Rider was ahead of Axel – after a few strokes, she saw Axel slipping behind. She could see the shark's fin but it wasn't very close. She wanted to stay with Axel and drifted towards him. Axel was tiring.

Rider called, "Float on your back, and I'll tow you in."

She put an arm around Axel's back over his arms, bent it over his upper chest and held onto his T-shirt, and did backstroke with her other arm.

"Kick your legs," she said.

She'd been taught to do this in still water, but the waves were breaking directly on their upturned faces. This was unpleasant. They both wriggled round to swim freestyle, with Rider still holding tightly onto Axel's clothing. Jeff was swimming out to them; he grabbed Axel, leaving Rider free to swim with both her arms. Before long, they were able to plant their feet on the sand.

As they clambered up the beach, a lifesaver came over to see how they were.

"I did not have to rescue people because everyone swam in well ahead of the shark," he said. "The patrol boat was between the swimmers and the shark, watching the situation."

The children gathered on the beach for a late lunch of sandwiches and fruit drinks, which Jeff brought in a picnic basket. Katie had to be called over; she was clutching a small box of shells to her chest and dragging a large container of seaweed. They ate ravenously while recounting the shark story. Katie was throwing her crusts to the seagulls, who arrived in hordes.

"I wasn't rescued by you," said Axel indignantly in response to something Rider said. "I was swimming in perfectly well on my own."

"I know," said Jeff, "but we were anxious about the shark. Everything people did – Rider, me, the lifesavers – was out of love."

They asked Katie more about what she was planning to do with the shells and seaweed. She said, "Venetia is going to show me how to make jewellery with the shells. My mum will cook the seaweed for a meal. You only have to wash seaweed and you can eat it raw. Or if you want to keep some of it, you dry it."

"What will you cook?" Rider enquired.

"Um. Seaweed soup and seaweed salad. Maybe put it in a stew, or have seaweed spaghetti. We'll invite you all over for lunch."

Rider and Axel both went "Urgh!".

"It's very good for you," said Katie defensively and no one could disagree with her.

Lunch was over.

"Can we walk around to the rocks and look for rock pools?" said Axel.

He wanted to remain on the beach until the last possible moment. The others said, "Yes, yes. We vote to stay."

The tide had receded, leaving little pools in rocks over by a headland. They walked on the rocks with bare feet, feeling the rough, uneven edges, and trying not to lose their balance. Peeking and prying in rock pools, they saw bizarre creatures: spiky sea urchins, sea anemones that sucked your fingers with waving tentacles, and all kinds of crabs that scurried to hide in dark corners. Suddenly, foam flew up in the air right in their faces.

"Oh! Oh! Oh!" A wave crashing in below two rocks was forced upwards between them and landed *splat!* on them and a crack that you could fall through.

They found a large pile of seaweed on the way back. Axel threw some seaweed at Rider and Rider tossed some at Katie. Soon, they were having a seaweed fight, slinging clumps and thrashing one another with long strands of it while laughing and screaming: "Take that, you silly goat!"

"Who do you think I am…stupid Old King Cole?" (his last teacher).

"Make way for mad Margot, I'm going to shoot you with my super kazoo!"

"That would be Kalashnikov?"

"Watch out, I'm farting – here it comes!"

Then, Rider raced along the beach sporting a seaweed necklace, waving her arms in the air and shouting at the seagulls like a madwoman, with Axel and Katie pursuing her in zigzags, bumping into and trying to knock each other over.

On the road home, the sun looked larger than normal as it sank towards the horizon, bathing the trees in an orange glow. Axel said that people believed the sun was getting bigger and would dry up the oceans. They would watch the shoreline to see if it was receding. Jeff said it wouldn't happen until after the human race died out.

"How long will that be?" asked Katie.

"It could be a million years. But humans are in danger of letting the temperature rise too high."

As they drove on, dusk deepened to night and they saw the aurora or southern lights fill the darkness, as it often did, with shimmering, diaphanous curtains of pink and green that seemed to blow about in the wind. They stopped and got out of the car to stand and stare, in wonder and awe at its lofty beauty. Jeff knew it was caused by solar radiation in the face of a decrease in the Earth's magnetic shield, the sign of an aging planet.

When everyone was seated back in the car and the car was moving on, there was silence. Only the driver was still awake.

After delivering the three tired and sleepy friends to their beds at home, Jeff made a torchlight inspection of his property before closing up for the night. He sensed there had been a disturbance while he was away: things were knocked over and the dogs had been barking and pawing the ground at the end of their tethers. The tool-shed door was banging in the breeze when it should have been locked. Casting his torchlight around the tool shed, Jeff discovered that some of his tools, which were usually clipped onto the wall, were missing. Of course, Rider could have borrowed the tools, but she was supposed to return them after use. Jeff felt sure that someone had been there, looking around.

At the first opportunity, Jeff asked Rider about the missing tools.

"I didn't take them. I always put them back."

"Do you think that boy, Gav, got into the tool shed after we forgot to lock it?"

"He could have. He picks up things that people leave lying about. He's always snooping while pretending he is visiting friends. By the way, I heard someone coughing outside in the night."

"That was the kangaroos – it's the sound they make,"

Rider was thrilled she had been to a sandy beach and surfed the waves. It was what she had always wanted. *The sandy beach is too far away for Jeff to drive me there often,* she thought. *But I have an interesting life with Jeff and new friends and things I have never done before. I can see the ocean every day.*

She asked Katie, "How was the seaweed you took home – yum, yum?"

"It wasn't so good," said Katie, clutching her stomach. "It would take a professional chef to cook it. The shell necklace was more successful."

The Visitors

Jeff and Rider did not expect to find the kind of visitors who turned up at their place one morning.

The dogs were barking over by the waterhole. Jeff went outside and saw two adults with two children there, half hidden by bushes. They were washing their faces and hands and drinking the water. Jeff called the dogs off and the people came out into the open. Their clothes were threadbare and dusty. They might have been walking a long way. The children were younger than Rider.

Jeff shouted, "Hoy! Can I help you?"

The people just stared at him and did not speak. Jeff gestured to them to come to his outdoor table. He sat down there himself.

The visitors walked over and sat around the table. They spoke a few words to one another which Jeff did not understand. They did not speak English!

By this time, Jeff was joined by Rider, who was on her way to tie some fallen tomato plants to their stakes. She had several pieces of string for the job.

Jeff pointed to himself and said, "I am Jeff," many times and Rider followed with, "I am Rider." The people did exactly the same and told their names. Now, there was a more relaxed atmosphere.

"Can you entertain the foreign visitors while I make tea?" said Jeff. "They will be less fearful of you because you are young."

So, Rider tied together the ends of each of the pieces of string that she was holding and made all sorts of string figures in her hands, like cat's cradle, cup and saucer, moth, star, parachute, and ladder, and taught the children how to do it.

When Jeff returned with tea and biscuits, the visitors consumed them with great gusto. They were very attentive to the globe of the world he had brought. Jeff pointed to Australia and said the word many times, pointing to himself and to the ground. Then he pushed the globe over to the man and woman. He thought they would indicate which country they were from. After turning the globe for a while, they pointed to Brazil, in South America.

A few moments later, Rider said, "I can't remember their names."

Jeff said, "I think the man was called Bruno."

Rider and Jeff thought it would be best to find things to do and to amuse the children. They took the family to see the animals. First, they went to the chickens to collect eggs for lunch. Rider had baby chicks, little balls of cheeping yellow fluff only a few days old, and the children loved holding and stroking them. She showed them how to make a hen go to sleep, by putting her head under her wing.

Jeff harnessed Caesar, the horse, to an old-fashioned plow that Rider hadn't seen yet and walked up and down the paddock to plow it. Next, he attached the cart and everyone got on board and drove the horse around the paddock. Rider brought apples and carrots straight from the garden, which she ate with the children at the same time as feeding them to the horse. The children fed the horse too, pulling back their fingers quickly when they saw the big teeth, in case they were bitten.

"Ooh, ooh!" they said, and giggled because the horse's mouth tickled.

Jeff fetched the hand shears in order to demonstrate sheep shearing. They all laughed and laughed as Jeff tried to seize Ivana the sheep, who always dodged away at the last minute. Having finally caught her, he did a little shearing. He handed the shears to Bruno and his wife; one of them held down the sheep while the other cut the wool. The sheep struggled to be free. She ended up a funny sight because of her uneven haircut. She was glad to run away when they let go of her.

Jeff thought his guests might like to use the bush shower while the sun was hot. He brought them soap and towels, and clean sets of old clothes to wear. Rider showed them how to operate the shower. She then went in to help Jeff prepare lunch.

In the afternoon, Jeff got together his old books that had illustrations. Some of them were children's books. Surely his foreign visitors could find things of interest to them.

The two children were particularly attracted to pictures of animals. With crayons and paper, they began to draw the weirdest creatures anybody had ever seen. They were like the ones in picture books where the pages are cut so you can join the top half of one animal with the bottom half of another.

"They have different animals in Brazil," said Rider.

When they got tired of drawing, Rider made paper planes with them, and soon they were throwing paper planes all over the room, with much laughing and jumping around.

Jeff was busily engaged with the adults in naming things in the illustrations. The visitors were trying to learn English. They picked up a paper plane and pointed to themselves and the plane.

"They came by plane," said Jeff. "They are 'plane people' who fly here without permission and land in the centre of Australia."

"Yes, yes," said Bruno. "People, people, people." He pointed to the middle of Australia on the globe. He traced a line with his finger going east.

"What happened to the people?" said Jeff.

Bruno could only wave his arms in all directions. But he held up photos he had found in the books of Aboriginal people who were eating food from trees, and digging in the earth to find grubs, roots, and water.

"These people helped you," said Jeff.

"Yes, yes," said Bruno.

"Was it too hot to live in Brazil?" asked Jeff. He fetched a box of matches, struck a match, and moved the flame towards Rider's bare arm. Rider shrank back and said, "Hot, too hot."

"Yes," said Bruno. "Too hot Brazil."

As it was nearly time to milk the cow, Rider and Jeff thought they would first take the visitors to see the food trees, in case they recognized them. They immediately started to eat different parts of the trees, like connoisseurs.

Everyone watched Rider milking the cow into the pail and dipped their mugs in for a drink.

Jeff decided to accommodate the family in the shed overnight as the weather was calm. He and Rider dragged over old mattresses and blankets for them. They could use the outside toilet.

Jeff wrote down his name and address for the visitors.

"I want to tell them not to say to others that they are plane people, but I can't think how to communicate it," Jeff said to Rider. "I fear people will discriminate against them, or cause them harm."

By morning, the foreigners had departed. They would find a run-down house to live in near Woogoo. Jeff and Rider decided to be their friends and seek them out.

There was another visitor. A man was patting the horse over by the back fence. It was the government inspector prowling about to examine the stocking rate on Jeff's land.

"Is this your horse?" he asked Jeff.

"Yes, I'm running it on an unused block of land."

"You can't keep it on a block where the food trees are not being maintained and protected by the owner. You are only allowed to have two fully-grown, large, herbivorous or hoofed animals on your own five acres, plus one baby animal from time to time. You have a month to get rid of one of your large animals, the sheep included." He tore off and handed Jeff a signed ticket.

"Why do you have these rules?" said Rider.

"Because it is now so hot and dry in Australia, we must promote plant cover that humans can eat and discourage them from having animals that damage the land. It is a better and cheaper diet for people to eat more plants and less meat."

After the inspector had gone, Jeff explained to Rider, "This means I'll have to sell Caesar the horse, as I would like to keep the cow and the sheep. Would you mind?"

Rider said she wasn't very interested in riding the horse.

"I'd rather ride a kangaroo," she said bumptiously. *That would be a bumpy ride!* "What will happen to Caesar?"

"The riding school in Woogoo might have room for a horse in return for free riding lessons. If it was a cow or a sheep, the local butcher would kill and freeze it, and give us so many vouchers for free meat. But I prefer to have milk and wool. After all, the cow satisfies our needs for milk, cheese, butter, yogurt, cream and ice cream."

Jeff phoned Woogoo Riding School and they said they would have a vacancy for the horse at the end of the month.

Rider took a walk through the unused block. Very shortly, she saw, at a distance, Gav dragging something through the undergrowth that looked like part of an old motorbike. He disappeared into the trees. *What is he doing?*

A Boys' Gang

Rider and Jeff knew there were many runaway boys at the time they lived, who sometimes joined gangs and roamed the countryside. They felt that they had no place in society because of their lack of skills and possessions to barter. They went in search of a way of life that would replace the old society of paid work, which had so disastrously shrunk with the exodus of people, mainly middle-aged people, to Greenland. It seemed they always had to learn from elderly people.

One morning, a gang of four teenage boys arrived at Jeff's place on their motorbikes, looking for food and water perhaps. The leader of the group was Steve, and the others were called Tony, Heath, and Zac. Jeff, like most adults would have done, tried to think of ways he could be helpful to them.

As soon as Rider came out to talk to them, she noticed their solar-powered motorbikes and said she was looking forward to owning one. The boys pointed out that she would have to wait until she was sixteen to hold a license, which dashed Rider's hopes yet again. But seeing the lightweight tents and sleeping bags attached to the back of their bikes,

Rider said she had been on a journey too. The boys asked her about it.

Jeff brought out a tray of drinks and insect biscuits for everyone.

"I wouldn't like insects," said one of the boys. But they all had a go at eating them.

Jeff took the boys on a tour of his intriguing property. They wanted to ride the horse and the cow bareback, to test themselves against the animals. Caesar, the horse, was agreeable for a while, and then dispatched the rider onto the ground pretty easily by making a sharp turn and stopping suddenly. The cow was disturbed by having someone on her back, and would only run forward a few steps and then pause to graze or to moo disconsolately.

Jeff thought the boys would like to hear about the crocodile he had killed near the dark, boggy waterhole. They immediately started searching in this place.

"Ouch!" shouted Steve, who was beating the bushes. It was an echidna. Everyone rushed over to see, and it was two echidnas; one of them was mating the other. The male was trying to climb up the back end of the female, who presumably had flattened her spines so as not to spike him. But she kept shuffling forward so that he fell off, and he had to try again and again.

Because of the hunting instincts of the boys, Jeff remarked that rabbits were an easy meal for humans and that you could kill them by throwing at them a stout stick, about two feet long, or a boomerang. The boys spent the rest of the morning practising throwing a stick at a target; however, they could not find a single rabbit. The rabbits must have run away to hide from all the visitors. At last, Jeff said he had a dead rabbit he wanted to skin and clean for dinner, and he described how to do it as he proceeded.

"In case the rabbit meat isn't enough to go around," said Jeff, "I have a small snake up my sleeve. You can eat venomous snakes."

The boys looked shocked, not only at the idea of eating a snake but thinking for a moment that Jeff literally had one up his sleeve.

While having lunch at the outdoor table, Jeff got the boys to eat different parts of the food trees, and to realize that they stored water and shaded you so you could survive in the outback. You were allowed to enter private property to eat food trees, but not to light fires or harm the stock.

"We learned about food trees at school!" chorused the boys, when they managed to get a word in edgeways.

Jeff and Rider found out that these boys mostly came from Sydney. They were both curious about what life was like there. The boys said that many families in Sydney had moved, because of rising sea levels, to live in suburbs on the inland side of the city adjoining open land that could be used for small farms. More city buildings were vacant because the professional people and workers in them had migrated to Greenland. An empty office was a dangerous place where builders and repairers often came to steal parts of the building in the day, and where criminals and down-and-outs lodged for the night.

"I was always being sent to mind our plot of vegetables," said Heath. "It was boring."

"Better than scrounging in skyscrapers for office equipment and building materials, where you could get killed and no one would care," replied Zac. "There were no police around."

"The train and bus services had been cut too," said Tony.

Jeff asked: "Wasn't there manufacturing and industry?"

"Yes, in a different part of the city," said Steve. "I used to go out to look for a job, but they were always laying workers off. People went there to buy goods at the factory door, as few goods were shipped anywhere."

In the afternoon, Jeff wanted some repairs to his shed. In a short time, the boys were at work and helped finish the job. They sat around afterward, admiring their workmanship.

"What if you need to purchase new solar panels for your bikes?" said Jeff. "Maybe you could do repairs for someone."

"In Sydney, we can find work, but it could be done by robots," Zac responded.

"There's manual labour," said Heath.

"Couriers and security officers," said Tony. "But you can't progress to anything much."

"That's why we prefer to ride about the country," said Steve. "And go to Sydney when there's a party or dance on."

Rider chipped in, "Do you fight with other gangs?"

Steve said, "If they fight us, we have to defend ourselves. We try to get away from them and go to a place where there are lots of other people because they won't fight us there. There are bad gangs, but most of us are good gangs."

"Watch out for bad gangs coming to your place," said Tony. "They are set on stealing weapons, tools, and food."

The boys showed Rider scars they had from fighting them, mainly from knife wounds. When they encountered these gangs on the open road, they had to head fast for the nearest town.

"You need to go to technical college and train," said Jeff.

"What reward would we have?" said Zac. "We would have to go back to living with our parents. Mine always put me down."

"Or pay rent in Sydney; they are starting to charge rent there now," added Heath.

"You could go to the Tech college in Woogoo," said Jeff. "You could find a cheap house there for all of you to live in." The boys lapsed into a thoughtful silence.

"You could then go to Sydney to get jobs," continued Jeff. "A lot of the jobs in Sydney are done in Woogoo free of charge by the community or Tech students in training. In Sydney, they have enough money to pay people. Multi-skilled people are a better option than robots."

Rider listened intently to the conversation and said, "In Woogoo, the Tech students fix all sorts of things for work practice, like roofs that have blown off and potholes in the roads. That's how they pay for their training."

Jeff said, "Whatever you do, don't start taking drugs and ruining your lives. I have heard there are bad people around, kidnapping children to work in the drug trade."

"We've come across those people and avoid them," said Tony.

I like Tony, thought Rider. *He's a caring person.*

For relief from Jeff's well-meaning lectures, Rider offered to demonstrate her martial arts moves and the boys said they would teach her the wrestling they had learned. These displays lasted for the remainder of the afternoon.

Jeff invited the boys to sleep in the shed for the night, after dinner. They could use his non-flushing outside toilet. Determined to impart more bush knowledge, Jeff showed them how to collect drinking water by tying a shirt over a bunch of foliage. By morning, this would be saturated with dew which could be squeezed into a receptacle. Then, Jeff placed a container in the centre of a hollow, with a piece of cloth over it dipping slightly in the middle. The cloth would drip into the container.

"You'll be able to clean yourselves afterward with damp cloths," said Jeff. *Boy, when is this going to end?* the boys thought.

"Can we have hot showers in your bathroom instead?" asked Steve. "We haven't been able to get a shower for a week!"

"Of course, you can," said Jeff, who was a kind person, and he ushered them into the house. Generally, boys didn't care much about washing, but there were limits.

At daybreak, the boys were making tracks. The air rang with the sound of engines being revved. Vroom, vroom!

"Would you like to go off in a gang in a couple of years?" Jeff asked Rider.

"I think I'll train at the Tech first," said Rider. But what she thought was: *If only I had a solar-powered bike, I might go. And I hope I'm going to see Tony again.*

The next day, Jeff and Rider read in the newspaper warnings about people in cars, or on motorbikes, who kidnapped children. This only happened on lonely roads, although sometimes also on deserted streets in Sydney. The children would be imprisoned and put to work in the illegal drug trade.

Fight in the Mangroves
and an Accident

In the winter, the cyclone season had ended. The weather was mild, with a little more rain. Jeff and Rider grew winter vegetables and were still producing nearly all their food. They didn't have so many visitors. It was better to work indoors.

They learned how to make wooden toys and puzzles for children, using a jigsaw. The toys, such as a train engine, were made in brightly coloured pieces that could be fitted together and pulled apart. Jeff and Rider could barter them anywhere because all people wanted well-made toys for their children and grandchildren.

Jeff and Rider took up fishing from the jetty once a week so that they didn't have to barter for fish. It was slow going to catch enough of them. In the mangroves, they found crabs and prawns too.

Often at Woogoo, dolphins appeared in the shallow water around the jetty. People would wade out to let them brush past their legs, and stroke them. Or they would toss to them from the jetty the tiddlers they had caught, which were too small to take home and eat. Children liked to throw the dolphins a beach ball, and some of them would swim in pursuit of the ball and bring it back and wait for it to be thrown again. These particular dolphins were not wholly wild animals.

While Rider and Jeff were out on the jetty, they talked with a lot of people. Jeff seemed to be very taken by a special lady who came to fish. They were surprised to meet up again with Tony from the boys' gang. He had left the gang for the time being and had gone home. His family lived on a small farm, just outside Woogoo. Tony showed Rider how to cast her fishing line in a more professional way. He said he didn't know what to do in the future.

Rider asked him, "Would you like to go fishing on the deep-sea trawlers, and bring in loads of fish? Someone offered me a job in that field. It's laborious work."

"Maybe."

"I would never catch and kill dolphins and whales though. Dolphins can save people from drowning."

"Dolphins and whales are not fish, and they are protected."

"I know. A group of people in Woogoo are against the dolphins because they eat the fish that people might catch. But there's nothing they can do. There should be more fish farms."

"That's a good idea. Maybe we could have a fish farm on our property."

"I hear you keep pigeons."

"Homing pigeons and they are very intelligent animals too. I train them."

Rider felt that Tony was reserved towards her because of their age difference. Tony was sixteen.

One day, Tony was talking about how he might go to the Tech college because Jeff had recommended it. Rider told him about the bully Gav, who was the only person Rider knew at Tech.

"Gav said to me 'You're thin and scrawny like a chicken, and the boys at Tech would pound you to mincemeat in a few seconds,' and other things like that."

"That's rubbish," said Tony. "The Tech boys would not do such a thing without good reason. How old is Gav?"

"Fifteen."

"He was preying on you because you are younger and smaller. He wanted to lord it over you and make you afraid of him. He's probably fearful of the boys at Tech who are bigger than he is. Perhaps someone in his family treated him badly."

Rider heard more stories about Gav. She learned that his family was poor, with many children, and he stole things for them. One day, as she was looking for edible shellfish, she saw Gav on the edge of the mangroves. Gav was resting nonchalantly on one leg, leaning on a tree, and staring at her. There was no one else nearby.

"Going to catch your seafood dinner, Rider?"

"I am."

"There are nasty things in the mangroves, waiting to poison people."

"Okay."

While she was thinking how to deal with Gav, she took her sling bag off her shoulder with fumbling hands and put it on the ground. She said, "I don't care."

"You don't care!"

Gav bent down quickly and picked something like a small reptile out of the mud. He said, "Here, take this for your bag then," and threw it at Rider's chest.

Rider ignored the provocation and searched in the mud for a crab. Just as she pulled one out, Gav lurched forward and swiped it from her hand.

"I'll have that one, thanks."

Rider thought she might leave before worse happened. Gav said, "I hear you do Judo classes."

"So what? Do you want me to show you some moves?"

"That would be good," replied Gav confidently.

He thought he could thrash Rider any time because he was bigger. *Yeah, clobber the little bugger.*

Rider immediately submitted Gav to a standing arm lock and held it a few seconds before releasing it. It seemed like an eternity.

Gav made a sound like an animal growling, "Grr," and swung a punch at Rider, which caught her in the chest. Rider went "Erf" as her breath was knocked out for a moment. She tightened the muscles in her arm and hooked it upwards. Her clenched fist collided with Gav's jaw and Gav's head was thrown back.

Rider was frightened of carrying on because she thought Gav would beat her. She turned away and ran further into the mangroves. It was difficult to run since she had to pick up her feet over the mangrove roots, and the muddy ground sucked them down. Just then, she remembered how she used to run from her older brother and surprise him by making a sudden left or right turn so that her brother would stumble forward and sometimes lose his balance and fall.

Rider glanced behind quickly at Gav charging at her and could see that he was clumsy and heavy on his feet. She dodged suddenly to one side and Gav found it hard to turn, stumbled, and almost fell and then corrected himself. Rider made a sharper turn to the other side, and this time Gav tripped on a mangrove root and shot forward to the spot where Rider had been standing only moments earlier. Gav's face and hands landed in the mud first, so that they were covered in oozy, sticky goo.

While Gav, with mud in his eyes, was trying to get up, Rider ran out of the mangroves, collected her bag of shellfish, and made her way to Jeff's parked car. She wondered what Gav would do to her next, after being subjected to such indignity. What was simmering and stirring in the dark recesses of his mind?

A few days later, Rider crossed paths with Gav at the cricket ground. She perceived that Gav was limping. Gav turned his face away as if he was engrossed in a game that was being played, and he obviously did not wish to speak to Rider. Rider was reluctant to mention anything about their fight.

Weeks later, Rider came across Gav again when they were fishing on the jetty with other people present. Gav wasn't limping, but he was wearing glasses which Rider had never seen him wear.

"Hello," said Rider amiably, "I didn't know you wore glasses." She thought Gav would be less likely to pick a fight with glasses on.

"They've only just been prescribed."

For once, he sounded like a normal person. But then he turned around and said, "Watch out! I'm going to get back at you for the fight."

Rider decided not to go fishing every time with Jeff. She wanted to do things on her own at home.

Rider went into Woogoo one day to do some chores. When she was walking along a deserted street that she was not familiar with, an old fellow jumped out from an alley and gave her a fright. He gabbled at her. His eyes didn't focus properly and his skin looked pock-marked. Food or something was around his mouth.

"I've seen you before," she said sharply. "Don't do that to me."

The man pointed at her and cackled. She couldn't help staring at him, his worn, dirty clothes. Then, just as suddenly as he had appeared, he disappeared behind a shrub as if he had never been there. Rider left straight away and walked quickly to the shopping centre.

At home that night, she had a nightmare about the man.

"He's a deranged idiot," said Jeff. "He's a bit crazy but has never harmed anyone that we know of. The council keeps him fed with Meals-on-Wheels, and don't reveal where he is housed in case people go there and annoy him. They don't know his real name but call him Gopher."

"But he gives you a fright, suddenly appearing and disappearing."

"He does that, and children are frightened of him. He picks on children who are on their own."

"He's not harmless if he frightens children, and throws stones at people."

Jeff was injured one day when he lost his balance and fell off the jetty. One step backward over the edge was enough to do it. He hit the water on his side, which partly softened his fall, and then crashed into some rocks just below the surface that should have been cleared from the area long ago. The hard, sharp edges of the rocks caused him grazing, bruising, cuts, and bleeding. An ambulance took him to the small local hospital for treatment and overnight observation. Rider was at home that day and received a message about it. She was told Jeff would soon be well, and to come to the hospital in the morning.

When Rider arrived in the ward, there was Jeff, sitting up in bed perkily and being cheerful, with bandages on one arm and one leg.

"I said I would give an arm and a leg to look after you," said Jeff in his jocular style. He felt fit to go home. The doctor dropped by to give the final word.

"Don't go falling off the jetty again, will you?" said the doctor. "We get a lot of falls off ladders when people are pruning trees, or working on their roofs. We're short of all medicines, medical supplies, and vaccines these days. In fact, some of our medicines that were locked away have gone missing, believed stolen. These drugs could be harmful in the hands of the wrong people."

Rider said, "Maybe Gav or Gopher stole the drugs."

The doctor and Jeff looked doubtful.

The doctor said, "Some, like the kidnappers, want medicines that drug people."

Jeff said, "I am worried about vaccines being available to protect dogs. Like rabies vaccine. Dogs infected by rabies, caught from rats, can pass the infection to humans."

The doctor said he had every reason to be concerned, and that humans would have to take care of themselves more and not expect to survive as long as they had. For a period of time, humans were able to replace their body parts and live for a hundred and fifty years, or more. This was now too expensive, and the specialists for this work were forced to live a simpler life like everyone else. He himself was retired and did most of his work free of charge.

When Jeff was next able to drive into Woogoo, he took an old set of surgical instruments that he had inherited to the doctor, as a gift. He knew that this would serve as payment for medical services. The doctor was delighted to accept them and said they would be useful for minor operations he did stitching people up.

Jeff recuperated in bed for a few days, while Rider did most of his daily chores for him. She did the cooking one evening and it was soon consumed. She said, "I cooked the dinner, and all you can do is eat it."

Rider hadn't told Jeff about the fight she had with Gav. When she finally decided to tell him, Jeff said he couldn't believe his ears.

"He had a fight with someone smaller, and a girl? What sort of a person is he!"

"He just thinks I look like a boy, and it doesn't matter. Anyway, I didn't get hurt."

Rider sent another letter to her mother:

Dear Mum,
I hope you are well. I'm still staying with Jeff. I work and do correspondence school.
Nothing much happened here. Love from Saskia.

Homing Pigeons

Rider's friend, Tony, bred white homing pigeons as a hobby, which his father had started. Rider went to his home on a farm one day and saw a dozen pigeons living in two pigeon houses. A pigeon perched on her hand to eat some seeds. She stroked its head; it was soft and beautiful. It would be fun to send messages by pigeon.

Tony liked nature, fishing, and being in the bush. He was a nice-looking boy and had a burnished complexion, like a person who had been out in all weathers. Before he joined the boys' gang, he used to go off into the wilderness on his solar-powered motorbike and sleep there alone. He told Rider he took a homing pigeon with him in a small cage as a companion and in case of emergency. He had a self-charging mobile phone but the pigeon was better. The phone might be outside the service area, or it might get snatched from him by a nasty person. He preferred having the pigeon, which had a message already attached to its leg and could be quickly released.

Rider immediately wanted to keep and train these intelligent pigeons of a special breed, who could find their way to their home base from miles away.

Jeff was not keen on the idea. "Keeping pigeons can make people ill, or cause allergy," he said.

Rider said, "I promise to keep the pigeon-house very clean, and not to handle the pigeons too much, or put them near my face." She got her way.

Rider and Jeff set about building a pigeon house for two pigeons. It was like a garden shed on stilts. It had a fine wire mesh floor above ground, with a tray under it to catch the droppings, wire mesh windows for light and air to pass through and little doors for where you placed the pigeon feed and water. There was a landing platform and a trap door by which the pigeons could enter the house and a perch for them to sit on when they were inside.

Tony had two young male pigeons he was happy for Rider to have. In exchange, he accepted one of several large cheeses Jeff had made and stored, which would last for a long time.

Rider was ready to train her pigeons, which she called Bert and Fred. It was hard to tell them apart. First, she had to keep them in the pigeon-house for four weeks and feed them twice a day. Then, she had to take each pigeon out in turn and push it through the trap into the house repeatedly, to teach it to use the entrance. It could not exit by its own efforts. After two weeks, the pigeons could be left outside to fly about, as they could recognize their home and knew how to enter it.

Now Rider walked with her pigeons, which were in a small cage, about one kilometre away from home, and released them to return home on their own. One time, she came across Gav on the edge of the road.

"What are you doing here?" she said. "Meeting up with your mysterious friends who live near a natural spring?"

"No. I'm looking for things that people have thrown away or dropped accidentally. I repair and sell them to help support my family."

"Don't you mean you steal things?"

"I only pick up what's lying on the ground."

"And what's in people's sheds if the door isn't locked?"

Gav shrugged and said, "Anyway, what are you doing?"

"Training my pigeons." She walked on quickly.

Gav shouted, "Be ready. I'm going to get even with you."

Rider acquired an old pushbike. With this, she was gradually able to take the pigeons greater distances in any direction before letting them go. The pigeons learned to fly home, where they knew desirable food was waiting for them.

Rider was cycling along a lonely road one day when she took a rest at the side of the road. She was admiring a fine old tree opposite, with a thick trunk. Suddenly, Gopher popped out from behind the tree and gave her a fright with his deranged behaviour. No one came along this road.

"Get away from me and don't follow me!" she shouted, jumping up, her heart beating hard.

He vanished.

Rider was surprised another time to see a car coming along the road towards her. Taking heed of the warnings about kidnappers, she turned her bike off the road and hid with it by lying down in some ferns. The car went past slowly and continued up the road. Rider knew there was a dead-end in that road, so the car would have to turn around and come back. She decided that the most sensible thing was to return home that day. She released the pigeon with an alarm message. She began cycling to beat the car.

Suddenly, she saw the car come up again behind her. It slowed down, drew to the side, and stopped. Two men got out and started running towards her. She cycled as fast as she could. The men appeared to be rather overweight and in poor condition for running. She sprinted on ahead. A close shave!

Rider avoided that road in the future. She warned people about it.

She visited Axel once to show him the pigeons before releasing them. The pigeons were cooing in their low, gentle manner. Axel wished he was allowed to keep pigeons.

"Would you send a pigeon to my place with a message?" he said. He didn't know anything about pigeons.

"No, it wouldn't fly there," said Rider. "It will only fly to its home where its food is. I could train it to fly to another place where it knows it has food, but I'm not sure how to do it yet."

She had already thought she would send a message to her mother like that, and she could send a message back by pigeon post.

Axel said, "Did you know Gav has gone away from Woogoo?"

"No. How do you know?"

"Everybody is saying it. They were always wondering what Gav was going to say or do next. He is the oldest in a large family, and they think he is trying to find a job somewhere."

Rider said, "He's trying to get away from Woogoo where he has a bad reputation."

"But he might want to earn money for his family too." Axel's dad had suggested it.

At last, the day arrived for Rider to try out her pigeons' homing instincts from a distance of about eighty kilometres. She arranged to travel pillion on the back of Tony's solar-powered bike. Tony would give her some lessons on riding the bike. They were going to camp overnight in the bush. They would take their food with them in bike bags: bread, cheese, carrots, cabbage, capsicum, apples, pigeon feed, and water. They would sleep in a two-man tent. Tony would take his own pigeon too. He knew a good place to go, a piece of bush on someone's farm.

Rider didn't speak much on the trip but enjoyed the wind blowing in her face and hair. When Tony drove his bike off the side of the road, they could see a path leading into the bush. Tony tried to drive along the path as far as he could, the bike bumping on stones and roots, and their faces lashed by branches growing over the path. They walked the last part to a clearing.

"This is the campsite," said Tony. He spread a tarpaulin on the ground and unloaded all their gear onto it, including their two pigeons, each in its own cage.

Tony said, "It's not lunchtime yet, so we could put up the tent and make a bush shelter." He said he often slept in a bush shelter under the moon and stars, without a tent, when the weather was fine. He was used to being on his own. The shelter was made with branches, some of which had to be cut. Newly fallen branches with leaves clinging on were preferable.

The two sat on an old log to eat their lunch. Tony said, "Many things I learned on the farm are also handy for living in the bush."

"My uncle used to advise farmers about agriculture."

"What happened to your parents?"

"I can't remember my father at all because he disappeared so early in my life." Rider faltered over the words, but she could say these things more easily nowadays. "I came to stay with my uncle this year for a change, and I can remain for as long as I like. His wife died and the rest of his family went to live in Greenland. My older brother recently left home as well."

Tony just said, "I dropped out of school too soon, so now I'll go to the Tech college."

"That's where I will be going."

"What will you study there?"

"Something to do with engineering. I'm interested in machines that fly. What about you?"

"Environmental science. Like building houses from waste material. When you come there, I'll be like an older brother to you."

They spent the afternoon exploring the land around them. There was an anthill taller than they were. In a creek bed, they could dig the ground with their hands, and water would fill up the hollow. They collected some food from food trees to eat later.

Tony had built a platform up a tall tree at an earlier time. They had to climb the tree to reach the platform. From there, a view of the surrounding countryside opened up and they could also see the farmhouse of the people who owned the land they were on.

"This is a fine lookout for seeing if a bushfire is approaching," said Tony.

When they returned to the campsite, Tony showed Rider how to rub sticks together to make fire. But he said they would not make a fire or cook, because it was too dangerous in the bush these days. The fire could easily continue to smoulder and get out of control. People used to light campfires to hold wild animals at bay, but in Australia, luckily, there weren't so many animals that harmed you. Snakes were shy, like the other creatures.

"I wish we still had koalas in the wild," said Tony. "They could cry like humans."

They got into their sleeping bags. It was a beautiful starry night. They lay in the shelter, looking up through the trees and when the leaves moved, the stars winked at them. The night birds sang plaintively a monotonous tune to put them to sleep. Occasionally, a mosquito buzzed them like a warplane, but they were too tired to wake up properly. Once Rider woke up, startled by a sudden gust of wind and a blood-curdling screech. Two eyes were staring at her from ground level, and two more slightly higher up. It was a possum with a baby on its back, scavenging for leftover food.

The friends were in no hurry to leave in the morning. As they were about to start for home, they released the pigeons. They watched them describe a half-circle in the sky, before departing. Rider noted the time.

"They might get back in one hour," said Tony, whose pigeon would fly to the farm, and his father would time it. "Eighty kilometres an hour isn't bad. We'll see if the pigeons beat us."

Tony didn't want to try and race the pigeons, though. Rider knew that Jeff would take the time of her pigeon's arrival.

Jeff did take note of the time. When Rider reached home, the pigeon was already ensconced in its pigeon house.

"Why do you think Tony likes me when he is older?" Rider asked Jeff.

"It's because you listen to him. You are accepting, and kind."

Am I? wondered Rider, remembering the fight she had with Gav in the mangroves.

The Little Fire

Rider woke up early one morning. Fidgeting with the bedclothes, she felt uneasy, on edge, as if something were wrong. The spring had been exceptionally warm. On the air that wafted in through the open window, she could smell dust or, more than that; was it smoke?

She slid out of bed and went outside. There was a certain restlessness in the air; the vegetables were rustling. Barker and Pogo were pacing about, sniffing things. They made snorting and coughing noises, and were rubbing their eyes with their paws. The pigeons were fluttering about in their house more than usual. Where was that acrid, smoky vapor coming from? It was on the wind. Rider licked her finger and held it up. It was from the northwest, the prevailing summer wind.

Rider dressed in her rough working pants and boots.

"There is a fire somewhere," she said at breakfast. "It might be someone burning off rubbish. I think I'll go and investigate it."

"Be careful," said Jeff.

Rider decided to walk northwest and was soon going through the small gate into the unoccupied bush property at the back of Jeff's. There was more undergrowth now because the horse wasn't grazing it, and it crackled underfoot. She thought she heard the fox – *Waa, waa!* – and saw it slink away into a hollow log. It probably had cubs there.

She came out onto a dirt track and veered farther to the right. *This must be behind Katie's block*, she thought. After a time, there was a small sign pointing to an old garbage tip. A tip could sometimes catch fire and burn. The council had opened a new tip now, but someone might be using the old one again. She chose the path to the tip.

When Rider reached the tip, she saw steam or smoke rising from parts of it. It was partly surrounded by eucalyptus trees and blackberry bushes, and she knew they could catch fire easily. As she stood staring at the scene, she saw a child approaching on a side-track. It was a boy of about six or seven years, carrying a bucket half full of water. He took no notice of her and poured water on a place that was smoking.

"What are you doing here?" asked Rider.

"I was playing with my friend on the tip and we lit a fire, but we are putting it out."

"Where did you come from?"

"Johnson's house, my grandfather."

"Go back and don't play here. There's more fire than you can put out and it's dangerous."

Rider returned home for lunch, and to tell Jeff about the tip. Jeff said he knew about the old unused tip and would inform the fire brigade about its present state so that they would douse it with water to keep the fire under control, which they did once in a while.

"Sometimes, the tip catches alight because of spontaneous combustion. This can happen if someone digs or stirs up the flammable material in it, and lets in oxygen."

Rider started back to the tip in the afternoon. She was worried about the children playing there. On arrival, she saw a different boy trying to beat out some small flames with a leafy branch. When she got close enough, she could see that the boy was almost encircled by flames, so that if he was beating in front of him, the flames were creeping up from behind. With a few strides, she was able to pick up the boy and the branch, "Gotcha!" and move them back to the safety of where she was standing before. She felt in the boy's pockets and drew out a box of matches, which she dropped into her own pocket.

"What's your name?"

"Fernando."

"You came from Brazil, didn't you?"

"Yes."

"And what's your friend's name?"

"Nick Johnson – I want to go back to him."

He cut loose and ran down the track that Nick had come from in the morning. But Nick was returning along the track with another bucket half full of water.

"Caught you both!" shouted Rider, as they came on up to her. "Now, you're not to play here. The fire brigade is coming this afternoon to dump a lot of water on this fire. Promise me you'll stay away."

"But what about Gav?"

"What about him?"

"He comes here and digs things up."

Nick and Fernando pointed to a pile of junk on the edge of the tip: part of a bicycle, car parts, all sorts of metal objects.

"What does he do with them?"

"Oh, he makes them into something. He repairs them. He makes money from them," the boys were chiming in, to each other. "He told us not to touch them, not to tell anyone. He'll come back."

"Look at this!" Rider said suddenly. "This is one of Jeff's spanners that went missing." She picked it up to take home.

"He brings stuff here too," the boys told her. "We will get into trouble if you take anything."

"He's a thief," said Rider, and the boys looked shocked and were silent. "By the way, have you seen Gav lately?"

"No, we haven't," said the boys, both at once.

"I know. That's because he went to Sydney."

Rider made a mental note to tell Jeff so that he could come and claim his tools.

The next day, Rider caught up on her homework.

"Every time I turn off the computer, it lets out a groan as if it's sick and tired of me, and glad to be free again," she told Jeff.

Jeff went to the tip and collected his missing tools. He noted with satisfaction that the fire brigade had poured a large amount of water on the tip, which was no longer smouldering. No boys were in sight.

"That little boy, Nick Johnson, you mentioned," said Jeff. "His grandfather lives alone in his old house on a bush block and won't move. His descendants living in Woogoo pop out to see him now and then, take some food and do some housework. Probably, they leave Nick there sometimes for company. I'll phone them to explain about the danger from the tip.

"You probably saved Fernando's life."

Rider heard there was to be a motorbike race in Woogoo for teenagers the coming weekend, at the motorbike club. She always longed to have a motorbike. If you didn't own a motorbike, you could hire one from the club for a fee. She asked Axel if he was going to ride in the race, but he was not interested. Tony was too busy working on his family's property. He warned her about crashes and injury.

Rider told Jeff about the race, and what she had to do to qualify, and asked him for the fee so that she could book a bike before they ran out.

"You won't know how to ride it."

"I'm allowed to have one free riding lesson, which they always offer."

"Oh, I suppose so. As it's spring, you'll have to do extra work in the garden. You'll owe me a bit of the prize money if you win."

Rider managed to fit in her free lesson and, on the day of the race, she went to claim her bike and compulsory gear from the clubhouse. There, her own boots, helmet, goggles, and gloves were all accepted as adequate.

The outdoor track was immediately outside the clubhouse. Kids of all ages were gathering. Some were doing wheelies and generally showing off their skills to intimidate other riders. Some had coaches giving them advice. When Rider turned up to take her place on the starting line, she saw Gav there. He had also hired a bike to ride and was hoping to win the prize money for first place, no doubt.

A man came with the starter pistol and the riders jostled for their places. Bang! They were off. The dirt from the track was kicked up and hung in the air and dusted every face. There was a hum of engines, like giant mosquitoes. Some of the riders bumped one another and a few fell off their bikes. Rider had a tough time turning the bike, with one foot nearly on the ground. She managed to stay seated, but it slowed her down. She knew when the race was finishing from the screeching of brakes.

Neither Gav nor Rider won the race. Gav was slouching away in disgust when Rider next spotted him. She called out to him, but he just flung his arms out from his sides, flicked his hands, and kept walking.

Gav Pays Back

The fire that had begun in the old rubbish tip left behind a pall of smoke which lasted for days. Rider thought she would keep a check on the tip and Gav's pile of junk there. First, she had to ask Axel if Gav had returned permanently from Sydney, as Axel was the person who had told her Gav had gone. She went to Axel's place one day and described the fire at the tip.

"Would you come with me and check on the tip regularly?" said Rider.

"Yes. And I am interested in what Gav was doing there."

"But did you know that he came back from Sydney?"

"No, I haven't seen him."

Axel's mother invited them into the kitchen to have drinks and something to eat. Axel's family had a good veggie garden growing on their quarter-acre block, so his mother had chopped up lots of crunchy raw vegetables to munch on. She cut them into curly strings you could bounce up and down.

Axel said, "I think I'm getting taller than you."

Rider had always been a bit taller than Axel. She stared hard at him and realized that she wasn't staring him down anymore, but staring him up! They measured themselves against the doorpost and, sure enough, Axel was taller.

"You'll probably get heaps taller than me," said Rider, thinking that she wouldn't like that much.

Axel didn't want to crow over it. Rider challenged him to an arm wrestle and she won.

After eating and drinking, they set off. It was a nice day for walking at first. The weather became cloudy and thundery as they got to Jeff's place. Here, kangaroos had gathered at one spot and were eating cardboard cartons.

"Jeff must have taken Barker and Pogo for a walk, or the dogs would have chased them off," said Rider.

The kangaroos held the cartons in their front paws, like a sandwich.

"They love them. They must need more fibre in their diet," continued Rider. "If we have any cartons, we throw them out for them. We sometimes use cartons for plant protectors, and the kangaroos pull them off the sticks in the night and eat them.

"Rosellas are like that too. They stand on a branch on one claw, and break off a little spray of foliage with the other claw and hold it, like a hand, to eat berries off it." They looked around the trees, but couldn't find any rosellas.

"You sound like you are practising to be a tour guide," said Axel. "What are those yellow-faced birds on the ground screaming at us? Ki, ki, ki!"

"They are masked lapwings. That's an alarm call. They are protecting their eggs which they are hatching on the grass and don't want you to walk that way."

Rider and Axel continued on their route. When they reached the edge of the old, rubbish tip, it seemed as if it was getting dark already, either from dusk, or smoke, or the density of the eucalypt forest. They stopped before they were in the open space because they saw a figure bent over the blackberry bushes. Then they saw flames and smoke in the same place. What was the person doing? A man was raking leaves towards the flames, which were dancing up and down around the base of the blackberries. It was Gav.

Rider and Axel shot into the open.

"What are you doing?" they both exclaimed.

Gav turned and saw who they were.

"I'm putting out a small fire I found in the blackberries." He dropped the rake and picked up a branch and began beating the fire.

"You were starting a fire," said Rider. "You were raking leaves *into* the flames."

"Did you see me set fire to the blackberries? I was raking the leaves away from the flames."

Rider and Axel picked up branches and helped to beat out the fire.

"How could a fire start by itself?" said Axel.

"It could begin by spontaneous combustion in the rubbish," said Gav. "The council ought to spray these blackberries – they are noxious weeds."

"The fire brigade dumped water on the tip only a few days ago," said Rider. "I don't think the fire started from the tip."

Gav suddenly said, "I know where there is a hose attached to a tap on a property near to here. Wait till I come back."

He ran down the track leading away from them. Rider and Axel continued beating until they were satisfied that the fire was out. Gav had not returned, so they both went home.

Rider worried all night about the meeting with Gav, and whether the fire was starting up again. She went by herself to inspect the tip the next day. There, she found Gav sorting out objects from his junk pile.

"I told you to wait until I returned with the hose," he said when he saw her.

"We finished beating out the fire and went home."

Gav came up to her with a piece of rope in his hand, and suddenly grabbed her arm and tied the rope tightly to her wrist.

"Hey, don't do that!"

Without speaking, Gav went around her and caught her free wrist from behind her back, and tied it to the other wrist.

"What the—"

"I'm going to tie you to this tree."

The tree was immediately behind Rider and had a slender trunk. All this had happened so fast. In no time, Gav put the rope securely around the trunk and knotted it.

"What can you do now?"

"Don't be silly, Gav."

"This is paying you back for the fight you won over me. I was hurt, but you were not. And my pride was hurt."

"But you provoked me. You made fun of me. How are you going to hurt me?"

Gav was looking for something, and Rider saw him pick up the end of the hose from the edge of the tip, which had a slow stream of water coming from it.

"I'm going to hose you."

"Well, don't come close to me."

Rider realized her head was free and she could bend it down away from the water if need be. She didn't want Gav to be close enough to force water into her nose and mouth so that she couldn't breathe. Just at that moment, she noticed that there were many fluffy seeds floating around in the air and one landed on her cheek. It felt itchy, but she couldn't scratch it. Her nose started running. She hung her head so Gav couldn't see her face.

Gav began to hose all of her body. He moved the hose up and down. The water had such low pressure that it barely reached her, and Gav had to press his finger on the end to increase the force to squirt the water harder and make it reach her. Up to her neck and down to her feet. Up and down, up and down.

After a while, he had enough of it and tossed the hose to one side. Rider was sopping wet and shivering. She said, "Jeff will wonder where I am and come looking for me. I have to milk the cow at five o'clock, so he will come and get me before that."

"I was going to untie you anyway," said Gav, and began to unknot the rope, "Now I have shamed you, with your wet clothes sticking to your body."

Rider slipped free the moment she could, and was moving away. "I don't feel ashamed at all!" she shouted back, planting her feet firmly in the undergrowth, and gathering speed by leaps and bounds to a slow run.

When she got home, she tried to evade Jeff. She stayed outside behind a tree, listening to a blackbird whistling. It made a sound like a boy whistling at a girl. She hoped Jeff would go out to the shed, and she would then rush into the bathroom. No such luck. She had to walk straight in.

"All your clothes are wet!" Jeff exclaimed, "Get them off quickly. What happened to you?" in a jumble of words.

Rider gradually told him some of what had occurred. She avoided saying her wrists were tied. She said, "I'm not afraid of Gav because I can see his upper and lower limits. There is a limit to his bad behaviour, and there is also a limit to his good behaviour. Gav hasn't said anything nasty to me for a long time."

To the Tip Again

Rider said to Jeff one morning, soon after her episode with Gav, "I want to check what Gav is going to do with some rope he has lying around. It is quite a lot of rope."

"You might consider taking Katie with you for company. She only lives a short distance from the tip."

"All right. I'll go after school hours. But I am worried that Gav might say something nasty to her."

Rider mostly studied for the rest of the day. It was a warm and lovely afternoon, with no smell of smoke. When she arrived at the tip, no one was there. The little boys seemed to have been staying away lately.

Rider knew to turn east at the tip and try to follow a path to the fence at the back of Katie's place. She looked for the walk-through, which was two posts placed close together that stock could not get through, and squeezed herself between the posts. In the garden, Katie was batting a tennis ball attached to a stretchy elastic line. She said she would be glad to take a look at the tip if Rider was there, as her home would be under threat if a fire broke out. She called to her mother that she was going with Rider. They walked back along the path, Katie sometimes skipping.

Gav had turned up and was sorting stuff out again on his junk pile. Rider thought he had brought new findings to it. Finders keepers.

The two girls stood and watched him for a while. Katie giggled. Rider said, "If you don't mind me asking, Gav, what are you thinking of doing with that long coil of rope that you have?"

"A rope is very useful, Rider, it can be used for rock-climbing or pulling things along the ground."

There was a long silence in which the girls went on staring at him. At one point, he motioned them to stand farther back, as he was spreading his loot out on the ground.

"I'm going to make an animal trap with the rope. It will be placed over a deep hole, so mind you don't get caught in it. It won't be a cruel trap."

"But what for?" said Rider.

"Well, I could trap prey for food. My family is large and poor, and I'm trying to help them. I don't have to baby-sit the younger children so much these days, so I use my spare time to support the family."

Gav seemed to be in the mood for talking to them.

"What animals would you catch in the trap?"

"Everything that falls into it."

"People's pets? You would eat them?"

"Yes."

Rider didn't believe Gav would know how to trap animals.

Katie piped up, "If I came across any animals in the trap, I would free them!"

"Why did you come back from Sydney, Gav?" Rider said. "I thought you went to find work."

"I found work drug-dealing, but the police were after me."

"Were you kidnapped to work in the drug trade?"

"No, I went by myself."

Gav bent over to do things and ignored them after that. Rider and Katie took a tour around the tip to see what it looked like. They whispered as if in a church. No fire. They found the blackened space in the blackberries where Gav had lit the fire. They came back and watched him again.

"What do you want now?" Gav said, straightening up. "When are you off home?"

"You are a kind person, to do so much for your family," Rider said.

"Yes." He paused. "When you think of how they treated me."

"How was that?"

"My father left me in charge of the children and they mucked up, and then he thrashed me. It wasn't my fault, but I was blamed for it all the time."

"Oh, I see. So, what was your mother doing?"

"Huh? She had to go shopping, or to the doctor, or something like that."

"How did the children muck up?"

"Why do you ask me all these questions?"

"I'm just curious to know."

"Well, they jumped on beds, cut up clothes, dug up plants, threw dirt in the house, hosed one another, locked people out of the house, and everything. Now I'm making money for my father, he doesn't beat me. But he's always being lord and master over me. See this polystyrene carving I did of him?" Gav fished this out of his pile of junk. "I throw dirt at it, spit on it, punch it, and worse things when I am mad at him." Gav's face twisted into a grimace.

"Ooooh." *What were the worse things? – think of something else to say* – "Your father works as a labourer, doesn't he?"

"Yes, if you want to know – you're like a reporter on a newspaper. We never have much money, and sometimes go hungry. The children are suffering and that's why they muck up. I'm trying to earn enough for a kidney transplant for my brother. So now you know everything, little Rider." He glared at her, "What about you?"

"What about me?"

"Haven't you left your mother for a long time now? What does she think about it?"

"It's private."

"You are like me, really. With your secrets and lies. You tell lies."

Katie had been quiet and said nothing much all along. She was trying to hide behind Rider and pretend she wasn't there. As they were walking back to Katie's place, Rider told her that Gav was known to be a bully, and told her things Gav had said to her.

"You're not upset about anything Gav said to us, are you Katie?"

"No, no. I'm not upset."

Rider asked if Katie had come across Gav before.

"I don't think so. He isn't known of, in my class at school. Perhaps he has grown up more and has changed."

"He's had to grow up too young," said Rider. "Maybe he'll become more normal. From today, I don't think he's such a bad person. But keep your distance from him, won't you? He's a bit weird. And keep your tool shed locked at night or he might steal something."

Katie ran into her house to tell her mother about what happened.

The next time Rider went to inspect the tip, it was with Axel. They saw a young girl coming along the track that the children had used earlier. Rider recognized her as she got closer; she was the daughter of Bruno, the Brazilian.

"I've come to see the tip where Fernando was playing. I believe it was burning. He's not allowed to play here anymore."

"You can see the flames were put out by the fire brigade dumping water on it," said Rider.

The girl nodded.

"I remember you," she said. "We're worried at home about bushfires. Our derelict timber house is in the bush, and Dad's fixing it up. We have an old car to escape in."

"What's your name?"

"Daria."

"We don't see you about."

"I'm always studying. I began high school and take special English classes after school."

"You seem to be very serious about your work."

"I am. I want to be a doctor when I leave school."

"I want to be an engineer," said Rider, "But it's a long time till that."

Axel said, "I don't know what to be yet. I suppose I might be a nurse or a social worker."

Daria gave a quick glance at Gav's pile of junk nearby. "Pardon me, I must be going home soon," she said.

"We're glad Fernando's being kept safe from harm, and hope to see more of you," said Rider.

"Oh yes. I was pleased to meet you again." Daria sneezed, pulled a tissue from her sleeve, and blew her nose. "I get hay fever in the spring, not asthma."

She shook their hands, saying "Goodbye," and turned and walked away down the track.

"A very polite girl," observed Axel.

When she got home and said goodbye to Axel, Rider found out that Jeff had phoned the council to see if they had sprayed the blackberries at the tip by now. They answered that they had.

Jeff wanted to take Rider to the shops to buy a bra. She was growing and developing breasts. She didn't want or like breasts. Jeff had already helped her with her periods.

"I don't want to wear a bra. It would make me feel caged in," Rider said.

"Would you prefer to be a boy?"

"Yes, if I had been born one."

"I'll take you shopping and the shop assistant will help you with the right size. Or I'll ask Venetia to go with you."

"I'll go with you if you don't come into the shop."

So, Rider went with Jeff in the car and he sat in it while she bought a couple of bras.

"I won't wear them if I don't feel like it. Or I'll bind my breasts against my chest so they look flat."

Jeff muttered something unintelligible.

"Do you think I'm at all pretty, Jeff? My nose is bent to one side."

"Not much. It gives character to your face. You may have been a bit of an ugly duckling, and a tomboy who has late development, but you will grow up to be a beautiful swan."

Now, digest that, Rider, Jeff said to himself as he went to clean the toilet.

Camping

Rider and Axel were planning to go camping together sometime. Rider was woken early one morning by fairy wrens tap-tapping on the windowsill, catching spiders. She liked to call the wrens "little violins" because of the sweet sound they made singing.

"You'd better go camping in the spring because it's getting so hot already," said Jeff. "At this rate, we'll be staying indoors in the summer trying to cool down. I'll keep an eye on the tip while you're away."

They decided on the midterm break, but the children would continue camping longer if they liked it. Jeff would drop them off on a track that went into a largely forested area known as Brown Mountain. You couldn't really see a mountain but it was more like a high ground, spreading a long way.

They would take backpacks containing a waterproof one-man tent and a sleeping bag, both of which Jeff owned. Axel had his own sleeping bag.

"You could share the tent with Axel if he's agreeable. I used to sleep on the ground, but we'll buy some half-inch foam plastic that you can sleep on and roll up."

Their ordinary clothes, including boots, would be enough: a hat, long pants to protect from snakes, sun-block cream for Axel. Rider would take her compass, an old map of paths, some rope, matches, soap, toothpaste and toothbrush, and toilet paper. They had a couple of small saucepans for cooking, a billy for making tea, plastic mugs, plates, bowls, and utensils. For food, they were going to pack dried meat, cheese, dried fruit and vegetables, rice, macaroni, rolled oats, insect biscuits, powdered milk, tea, sugar, salt, and some fresh fruit and bread.

"Gosh, we don't even eat sugar and salt at home," said Rider.

"Well, you may need them for additional energy. And I'll put in some sultanas and nuts you can eat while out walking, also. We used to call that scrumpy. Don't forget you must get water from a creek once your small amount of bottled water runs out. Take the badminton set too."

Jeff drove Rider and Axel to the beginning of a regular track on Brown Mountain that was sign-posted *Brown Mountain Walking Track*. He pointed in the general direction of the creek and suggested they should camp near it for a couple of days, and fan out from it for their daily explorations.

"You can wash yourself and your clothes in the creek."

"Yes, yes," said Rider impatiently, making sure everything from the car was in her pack. They'd be glad getting away from Jeff telling them what to do.

"What's that rope for?" Jeff said.

"It might come in handy." *Wouldn't Gav get a shock if Axel and I pounced on him and tied him up with the rope?*

Jeff watched them trudge away.

After Axel and Rider located the creek, they went uphill a little way to find a suitable flat campsite. It was easy to erect the tent with two poles at each end and tent pegs to hold the ropes. They put their gear into the tent and finished up all the fresh fruit, bread, and bottled water for lunch. They gathered kindling lying on the ground, not far away, to make a fire later for cooking.

"We'll have to be very careful to see that the fire is out when we don't need it," said Axel.

They spent the rest of the day tramping about in the bush, using the compass for direction. One of them would walk a distance they believed was north and, after counting to twenty, the other would walk true north and see if they met up. If not, they would start shouting, "Cooee!" until they found each other not far away. After that, they set out a badminton court, put up the net and played a game. They tried skimming flat stones on the creek, but there was not a wide enough expanse of water.

"We won't need to wash in the creek today," Rider said.

Before dark, they got a fire going and managed to cook a meal. They fell asleep listening to the boobook owl crying *"Boobook!"* over and over, and the bellbirds continually ringing like little bells. In the night, Rider heard possums hissing at one another. They were going to have a fight.

When she woke up, it was very early and for a minute, she couldn't remember where she was. She turned her head and there was Axel, still sleeping. Outside, there was a dawn chorus of birds singing, calls of currawongs, the *cluck cluck* and *quack quack* of wattlebirds, the lovely carolling of magpies and harsh screeching of cockatoos. For a while, she lay and listened, but then wanted to get up and see everything, as if she hadn't seen it yesterday. Squirming out of her sleeping bag, she wriggled along the ground on her elbows and poked her head out of the flaps of the tent. Grass! With little insects fluttering in it – that's what the birds were looking for. She pulled herself up and out, stretched, and yawned.

She noticed the dirty saucepans littered around the blackened remains of the fire from last night and decided to take them down to the creek for cleaning. She softly half-slid down, using the bushes for brakes with her bare feet. *Ouch*! Some insect bit her foot. The water in the creek looked muddy and there wasn't much of it. She roughly cleaned the saucepans with her hands. She could see a blurry reflection of herself with short hair standing up in all directions. She went to find a different pool of standing water to wash her face in and took a billy full of water out of it first. There was an echidna in a small trickle between the pools. It was sitting and cooling down its stomach in the water, which Rider observed was moving past it. So, there was some water running from one pool to another.

When she returned to the tent, Axel was stirring and called out to her. He stayed in the tent, dressing, while Rider searched for their breakfast things.

"Let's just have rolled oats with sultanas, and I'll mix some powdered milk to pour on it. I think the water's all right to drink without boiling."

It took them a long time to have breakfast, get fully dressed, go to the toilet behind a tree, and put everything away again. Rider waited while Axel went down to the creek for his ablutions.

"Where will we go?" said Rider.

"What about the path that goes straight up? We missed it out yesterday."

Axel and Rider were walking up the hill behind their tent when they came across a kangaroo lying on the path and blocking their way. It had a pouch, so it was a female, and she did not hop away as they approached, in the usual manner of kangaroos.

"I wonder if she is sick or injured," said Rider. They came closer and were going to pat her, but the kangaroo suddenly stood up very straight and waved her paws above her head, stretched out her claws and hissed at them. "She doesn't want us to walk up this path."

The kangaroo dropped down again when they drew back. She had seemed to be limping. She used her legs to swish the sandy soil about to make a bed for her to lie in.

Axel said, "She is claiming that soft spot on the path for her own domain, so we are not allowed to come near it."

After walking around the sick kangaroo, they continued on up the hill into thick bush. At the top of the hill, they could barely see a view. They then came across a gully densely crowded with plants. You couldn't see the sky because of ferns with arching branches just overhead. It was like walking through a room or corridor. They ran about under them, parting the fronds of the ferns and saying "Boo!" and silly things, and giving each other a fright. Here, Rider noticed large orangey cones that looked like pineapples on some shrubs. They both examined them and thought they were fruit or nuts.

"They are seed cases," Rider decided.

Later, they came up to a little hilltop with rocks and a pine tree and, sitting on this, they could glimpse the sea. It was very hazy and they couldn't see the line of the horizon between sea and sky. If they squinted their eyes, they could just make out tiny boats and ships crawling like insects.

They talked for a long time and returned to their campsite at dusk. The sick kangaroo was still guarding her special site. They brought her a saucepan full of water from the creek and she drank it up avidly.

"When I was down at the creek, I heard a frog croaking, and I think it was the endangered green and gold frog," Axel said.

They went on down and listened, and tried to find the place in the rushes where the sound was coming from. *"Waa, waa, war, war, war."* They couldn't see the frog.

"We'll have to wait till tomorrow," said Rider. "We still have to make a fire and cook dinner before dark."

While that was happening, there was some thunder and lightning but no rain. They hadn't perceived that clouds had crept up on them.

In the morning, Rider followed Axel down to the creek. They listened.

"That's the sound!" exclaimed Axel. There it was: *"Waa, waa, war, war, war!"*

They tried to find the green and gold frog, dodging their heads from side to side as they stared at the rushes. But they couldn't see it. They rattled the rushes, and some frogs jumped out so fast from reed to reed that they couldn't identify them.

"I'm sure it's them," said Axel. "The Olympic team should adopt this frog for their mascot because of its colours, and draw attention to its plight."

They discussed where to go next.

"The sun isn't very bright this morning. The light has an orangey look that it might have when people are burning off, or there is a bushfire," said Rider.

"There's a lot of burning off now in the spring," said Axel. "I can see smoke around in the sky today."

They looked for a point where smoke was coming from, but couldn't find one. There was just generally a smoky appearance.

They didn't pursue the matter but kept it in mind that there might be a bushfire somewhere, not necessarily nearby. If fire threatened them, they could take refuge in the creek. They went on with their daily activities.

"Have you ever cleaned your teeth since you've been here?" said Axel.

"No, I completely forgot."

They went down to the creek together to clean their teeth. While they were there, they saw someone walking along the bank of the creek towards them. It was Gav. When he got close, Rider said,

"Expecting to meet your mysterious friends, are you?"

"No."

"Picking up tools and old junk lying on the ground?"

"No. I'm worried about some smoke I saw."

"Did you see it from your home?"

"No. I only go there last thing at night, and leave early in the morning."

"So, you're being like a watchman?" said Axel.

"I suppose so."

"Well, good luck to you," said Rider, as she and Axel set off for the tent, and their work clearing up.

"Do you think a fire started up from the lightning?" she said to Axel.

"It could have."

Fire on Brown Mountain

By this time, Jeff had noticed the same signs of fire. He phoned the chief volunteer firefighter to compare notes on the subject.

"Have you located a source for a fire, or is it just general burning off?" Jeff said.

"I know there are people burning off in the Brown Mountain area," said the volunteer. "I'll let you know if I find out anything new."

Later that day, Jeff heard that someone had perceived smoke coming from a definite point in the Brown Mountain area and was going to investigate it.

Jeff knew that he would have to go and find the children, because of the danger, and bring them back. Goodness knows where they had got to by now. They had his tent, but he could pack an old sleeping bag. He would take the dogs and, as Jeff walked with them along the paths on Brown Mountain, they could become sniffer dogs and search out the two friends. He would take a bag of Rider's clothes, clean or dirty, for the dogs to sniff.

He phoned Venetia to explain how he might be away for an indefinite time. She said she would check his house, feed the chickens, and keep the eggs the hens laid. She would keep an eye on the tip.

She said, "Don't worry about a thing here."

Jeff loaded everything into the car and drove to the start of the track at Brown Mountain. He said to the dogs:

"Here, Barker, smell Rider's jeans that she never washes. Mmm. Pogo, take a whiff of Rider's old socks that she won't throw out. Hey, don't eat them!"

They sniffed them.

The dogs raced out of the car and chased each other, looking for food scraps and rabbits. Jeff caught Barker and put him on a lead. This kept Pogo in his control, as well as free to work over a wider area of ground at sniffing. Jeff kept in his pocket a T-shirt of Rider's that they could sniff again. He was following the path that Rider and Axel took and he knew they would camp near the creek. That is unless they had decided to do something different.

"Where is Rider?" he was saying to the dogs. Barker and Pogo were content to accompany him, apart from some dashes Pogo made into the bush as a noise or scent excited him. The tent would not be far from the track as it came closer to the creek. At last, Jeff saw it on a flat ledge, walked up to it, but no sign of life. Well, they would be off on their adventures, of course. Barker and Pogo sniffed all around.

Jeff started to work the dogs from the tent over a progressively wider area. He kept giving them the T-shirt to sniff, pointing to the ground and saying, "Where is Rider?" In a while, the dogs found the kangaroo, lying down as usual, and frightened her into jumping up and taking some small awkward hops, dragging one leg, to get behind a bush. Jeff could see something was wrong with her and commanded the dogs to stay back. After that, Jeff ran out of ideas about how to train dogs and strode farther up the hill with the dogs at his heels.

Up there, Rider and Axel were climbing trees to try to sight any fires. This was giving them trouble as they weren't used to the particular trees. The eucalypts didn't branch till high up. They had some rope in hand to which they tied a stone and threw it over a branch. They had to repeat this many times to get it over.

Rider knotted a loop in one end of the rope, put her foot in, and looked enquiringly at Axel.

"If you hold onto the rope, I'll pull you up to the branch," said Axel. However, he was not strong enough to pull Rider off the ground.

There was a wattle growing beside the eucalypt that could be climbed some of the way before bending too much. Rider went up on it. She had the compass in her pocket.

Axel said, "You'll have to go hand over hand up the rope and hold on with your knees and feet somehow. If you fall, the wattle will break your fall, and I will run forward and try to catch you too."

Rider kept going. This was horrible. She didn't look down. When she got to the branch, she couldn't put her right arm around it enough and get a grip.

"Can you see a small offshoot on the branch near your left arm? Can you slide your left hand off the rope and get hold of it, and use it to help pull you up?"

"It might break. My right arm mightn't hold me while I do that. Oooo."

"Go!" shouted Axel, "Do it! I'll catch you."

With a tremendous effort, Rider did what he said, and pulled herself over the branch so that she was balanced half over one side and half over the other.

"Hurray!" shouted Axel.

She was able to pivot her body around and get one leg over the branch and lean against the trunk. She locked her legs together to be more stable and took the compass out of her pocket.

"This is a great view. The smoke is about northwest. I'll take an exact reading. It's 310 degrees." Axel wrote it down. "I still can't see where the smoke is coming from because of the trees. There is a clearing on the farther side of the smoke, so it might be a fire in the trees, or a burn-off just on the other side of them. We'll have to walk down there and see."

Rider spotted Jeff climbing the hill below them and cried out, "Hello! What a surprise!"

Barker and Pogo ran up in no time and were jumping up against the tree trunk and yelping.

"How do I get down?"

"Hold onto the rope and I'll lower it," said Axel.

Shortly, Rider was crying "Ow, ow!" as she was being scratched and stabbed by the wattle on the way. There were big hugs all round at the bottom. Rider was smacking herself because ants had got under her clothes.

"What happened to the kangaroo down below?" said Jeff.

"We don't know. She won't move from that place. She must be sick or injured," said Rider. "What can we do?"

"I'll phone the organization who deal with this sort of thing. They'll come and give her a needle to put her to sleep temporarily. It will take two men to carry her in a blanket to a vehicle. If possible, they will heal her and release her back into the wild."

Jeff said that he was going to take them home because of the threat of fire. They wouldn't be able to walk down the creek to see better where the smoke was coming from. He helped them take down the tent and pack their things. They carried all their gear along the track to the car.

When Jeff and Rider returned to their house, life went on as normal. There was no immediate emergency about a bushfire. Rider was catching up with homework. Venetia had kept an eye on their property and the tip and had seen no one there.

"I see you have taken some of my chickens as payment in advance," Jeff said to her.

"Oh yes, because you might have been away for days. I sold them for a high price because the one I ate tasted so good. I've been eating your vegetables too."

Jeff said, "Chickens raised at home on rich food taste better than the shop ones."

Rider resumed her guard of the tip. She didn't run into anyone. She looked curiously at the depot of things Gav had set up, wondering if there was anything there that she would like. He would have probably have hidden anything valuable. Maybe, if you sifted through the stuff in the tip, there would be diamond rings and real treasures. But she didn't feel at all like scratching and poking through it.

Then, Jeff received a call for volunteers to put out a small fire encroaching on the Brown Mountain reserve. They would have to drive in as far as possible in a steep, rocky area, and attack the fire with clearing, back-burning, beating and water until it was out. Rider was to stay at home on her own and look after the animals, but Venetia and Katie's mum would drop in and see that she was managing, or Rider could go around to their places any time. The dogs were to stay with Rider.

Before going, Jeff took Rider out for a treat at the Merry Wizard shop, café, and service station, which he thought they both deserved. They went into a section of the cafe which was usually reserved for truckies. It served them very large helpings at a low price.

"Mug or cuppa chino?" said the waitress.

"What's a chino?" Rider asked Jeff.

"Posh coffee."

"Oh." Jeff ordered a mug of chino and Rider a soda.

"Would you like to have homemade apple pie, with ice cream, custard, and cream?" Jeff said.

"You bet," said Rider. And that's what she had. All of them together. They both did.

"Into the Dam!"

Rider heard from Axel that a group of high school students, mainly boys, were planning to go into the Brown Mountain reserve to look for bushfires.

"What would they do that for?"

"They want to help put out the fire."

Rider decided to go herself and asked Axel to be her companion, but Axel's parents forbade him to go. No adults would have wanted untrained school students to fight a fire. But it appealed to the students as a heroic act. Rider thought like that too. She used to have dreams about rescuing people from fires.

Rider was supposed to be looking after the animals at home. She asked Katie to take over her job.

"If you just milk the cow once a day after school it will be enough. The cow will lower her milk output to suit." She showed Katie how to milk the cow.

Rider felt familiar with the topography of Brown Mountain because of her camping experience with Axel. She joined the other teenagers at the start of the walking track on the appointed day. They had all known where that was and had managed to walk there.

Some of the school students had rather poor provisions, whereas Rider knew what food to take. She had sensible warm clothes in her light backpack and was going to sleep on the ground under a shelter of branches. She took a pigeon in a little cage with a message attached to its leg, to send to Jeff's place to say where she was, especially if she was in trouble. She brought some pigeon feed.

The students had no fixed plan about what they were doing and started walking along the track in dribs and drabs, some walking faster than others. Rider chose her own direction, heading along the creek to look for her old campsite. When she reached it, she checked the uphill path where the kangaroo had been. The kangaroo was gone, but scuffle marks were still in the sandy soil where she had lain.

Dense smoke was coming from the northwest point of the small fire she and Axel had discovered earlier, which was what she expected. Somewhere down there were the firefighters, trying to stop the fire burning southeast over the top of Brown Mountain. The prevailing wind from the northwest and the uphill lay of the land would be making it more difficult for them.

At this point, Rider found herself alone, as the others had scattered into the bush. She would walk towards the fire, doing her own reconnaissance and keeping close to the creek. She and Axel had never walked down there. Eventually, as the smoke became more unpleasant, she returned to her campsite for the night and prepared her shelter. In the night, she was feeling frightened that Gopher might suddenly appear.

It was during the next day when she was retracing her steps of the previous afternoon that she met Gav on the edge of the creek. He said, "There is a boy lying on a rock ledge above here by the name of Wolfe, with an injured foot or leg."

Gav was filling a large tin mug with water from the creek, to take to the boy.

As they both scrambled up the rough ground to the ledge, Rider's mind went back to the conversation she'd had with Gav at the rubbish tip, which she'd been thinking about.

"I'm sorry you were so wronged by your family."

"Are you trying to gloat over me?"

Wolfe was still lying down and was glad to see them and have a drink of water. They helped him to stand up, but he found it painful to put weight on his foot. He tried a few steps, in which he swung the good leg forward quickly and dragged the bad leg up to it. It would take him a long time to go home hobbling or limping in this way.

"The trouble seems to be in your foot," said Gav. "Is that right? It looks swollen."

"Yes."

They got him to sit down, so they could look at his ankle and make him wiggle it a bit.

"It's probably just a sprain. Do you think so?"

"Yes. It hurts when I do that."

Rider took off the long-sleeved shirt she was wearing over her T-shirt and tore it into strips. She bandaged the boy's ankle firmly, which would help support it. They then tried walking with him a little way, but it was extremely slow. Gav said, "I'll carry you."

Gav is impatient, thought Rider.

Gav picked up the boy in his arms, and started walking, taking a less steep route.

"You're carrying a high school boy," Rider said.

"He's not heavy."

He was a small, skinny kid.

"I'm not in high school," said Wolfe. "I'm only eleven."

"So how many juniors are running around on Brown Mountain?" said Rider, to no one in particular.

When they came to Rider's campsite, she said goodbye to them.

"I'll take him to his home," said Gav.

"You should put him down to have a rest now and then."

"Okay, I will."

Gav then put Wolfe down on a rock at a higher level that he could stand on for a moment, and turned his back on him.

"Put your arms around my neck, and I'll piggyback you."

He grabbed the boy's legs so that they were over his hips and jogged off. *He'll soon be slowing down*, thought Rider, seeing the boy's foot being bumped around.

The following day, Rider did very little, feeling lethargic from breathing in smoke, until she realized she should be looking for children who were lost or could not cope. She shouldered her small backpack and picked up the pigeon in its cage. She walked on up the slope that she and Axel had traversed before, and did not find any children. Someone was calling from behind her and she turned.

"Axel! You said you weren't allowed to come."

"I know. But then I told my parents I was going to see you as you were on your own at home, and I might stay there. I met Katie, and she was managing okay with the animals. Then I left and walked this way, not meaning to go so far. I felt worried about you."

Rider told him about Gav and the injured junior, and how she was looking for others who might need help. They went on up the hill together, until they saw ahead the rock where they glimpsed the ocean. As they ascended, the scene that was gradually revealed to them was a number of teenagers sitting around on the rock.

"Welcome to Anzac Knoll," they cried out.

Rider and Axel scrambled up to the top of Anzac Knoll and sat looking at the view under the Lone Pine. The Lone Pine had been planted to commemorate the battle of Gallipoli.

"The soldiers were holed up there," said Axel. "They had a good viewpoint and defended it against the Turks so they couldn't advance."

"Did they all get killed?"

Nobody knew.

"We could defend it against the fire," said a boy. "The rocks here would protect us, and even the pine tree wouldn't catch fire."

"I wouldn't count on that," replied Axel.

The boys said they were going to return to Woogoo. They were hungry and thirsty. They were now avoiding the firefighters because they would get into trouble.

Rider and Axel decided to continue on the other side of Anzac Knoll, to go to Tony's farm. When they came out of the forested land of the mountain into the foothills which descended to the coast, they looked back. They could see, further to the north, a fierce blaze in the eucalypts around the side of Brown Mountain. The trees were bending over in the high wind.

"Look at the fireballs!" cried Axel. "See the round balls of fire leaping through the treetops in a strong wind! Sparks flying everywhere. Embers raining down. How could you fight that?"

"The fire has got past the firefighters in that spot," said Rider. "I hope Jeff is all right."

She decided to release the pigeon with a location message.

After a while, they found themselves following a dirt road. Tony's farm was somewhere here.

As they came nearer to the property, they could see the heavy smoke of a bushfire burning towards it. It was cleared land but threatened by grass fire. They were searching for the name of the property on the gate: Amaroo. They were glad to be on a road, which offered some protection from a fast-moving grass fire as long as it was stopped by the road. *Amaroo.* There it was, the name written on the open gate. They entered and walked along the driveway, ever nearer to the fire and thick smoke.

"We were mad to come here," said Axel.

"I can see their car," said Rider. "They haven't left yet."

Closer to the homestead, they caught sight of Tony. He was on a ladder, engaged in blocking the downpipes and filling up the gutters with water. Tony was a trained firefighter and was accepted by the volunteers because he was man-sized, and it was not thought he would be one of those rogues who lit fires. But he was needed by his father today to help save the property.

"How on earth did you get here?" he called out when he saw who was coming.

"We walked through the forest – we saw fireballs – it's much safer here," said Rider.

"You believe that? We were just thinking of leaving. Lucky you found us."

At this moment, Tony's father came up and spoke some words to Tony. He had opened all the gates so that the sheep, cows, and kangaroos could run from the fire. The pigeons had been let out of their cages to fly away – they would be disoriented by the smoke but would return slowly.

Tony called, "Come this way. It's too late to leave. We are getting into the dam."

Everyone – Tony, his dad, Rider, and Axel – got into the dam fully dressed, and waded towards the centre where it was deepest, and farthest from the fire, but still possible to stand on the muddy bottom with the head above water. Tony's dad had brought a wet blanket they were to hold up over them one hand at a time, to give the other arm rest, and they each had an old tin or plastic mug to bale water over their heads. That way, they would avoid some of the smoke and radiant heat which were the dangers.

"Where's your mother?" Rider asked Tony, who was standing beside her.

"She went into Woogoo earlier to be with friends and relatives," replied Tony.

Because Rider so loved native animals, he added, "We have two echidnas courting each other under the house, bumping into old building material all night which they will get under for protection."

The bottom of the dam was cold and very squishy, and Rider kept moving her feet and wiggling her toes, constantly thinking that yabbies were biting and nibbling at them. She could feel her head and raised arm getting hotter and was glad to change over to the other arm. She could use her free hand to pour water over her head. How good was that!

The bushfire was making a great noise now, like a roar; there was a strong wind, and the smell of smoke and burning increased. The fire was coming for the house, which was weatherboard and might burn down. It could reach the dam and go around each side of it, but the dam was too big for the flames to reach the middle. It seemed like an age standing there, concentrating on keeping up the blanket roof. Rider thought of the echidnas and felt relieved that they would be safe.

Then it became quieter. Still, they stayed there for a long time, not daring to come out. When they did eventually, they saw that the fire had missed the house. It had come close to the dam but passed without causing them harm. The mown grass around them was only singed. The garden shrubs and fruit trees had largely resisted the fire. The car was burnt, but not Tony's motorbike.

"What will you do about the car?" said Rider.

"We'll have our other car when the missus drives home," said Tony's dad.

At last, they all went inside the house for a rest and some food and drink. Soaked to the skin, they sat on the plastic chairs of the wired-in veranda to dry out. Tony's dad said, "We have to stay alert, watch and wait, too. The fire might be blown back."

He went outside again to see if there were any small fires burning in debris to extinguish.

Coming into the house a little later, he said, "Look what I've found."

It was Rider's small backpack and pigeon cage which she'd dumped beside the dam. They were undamaged.

When it seemed safe enough, Rider and Axel set out to walk to Woogoo by the dirt road. The fire had stopped by the road as everyone hoped, and some grass was still burning or smoking at the edge.

After a time, a large truck pulled up beside them and offered a lift to Woogoo. Rider and Axel climbed into the front of the truck and they were off. It was an old truck, like a great monster, grinding and honking its gears as it began to move. It was carrying a load of logs.

Farther along the road, there was a shower of rain, followed by a clear pink sunset, which turned everything into a bright magical green. The wind had changed and was blowing the smoke in a different direction. As they came into Woogoo, Rider and Axel could look down on the rooftops from their perch high in the truck.

Axel said, "I'm enjoying this because I don't live in a two-storey house, or on a hill."

"I wonder what your parents will say about your absence?"

"I'll tell them I couldn't find you at home and felt worried, so I went in search of you in the reserve. We walked and hitchhiked home, and I'll play down the part about being in the dam while the fire burnt around it."

Fire Threatens Woogoo

Over where Jeff was, the firefighters were doggedly battling the fire when suddenly, from behind their backs where the trucks were parked, a boy ran out of the smoke towards them.

"What are you doing here?" they called out, in shock.

"I got lost."

The boy explained how the school students had come onto the reserve to help the firefighters, but they had become separated.

"Get away," said a firefighter. "Try to direct any other kids you see away from the fire."

"We don't need anything like this," shouted another. "Some boys are going to be in trouble."

Jeff pointed towards the creek. "Follow the creek and it will take you back to the track that enters the reserve. We can't spare anyone to take you."

The fire was being fought by the fire brigade members combining with the voluntary firefighters. The fire brigade members were known to harass one another on occasion in these times when there were so many fires and not enough men to deal with them, so they would sometimes conflict with the volunteers too. Of course, they would try to cooperate. An aspect of the volunteers was that a young man or teenager would sometimes turn rogue and light fires that he wanted to fight, hoping that no one would find out.

"One of these kids has lit the fire!" called out one of the men.

"We shouldn't have any female firefighters," said another. "The women should be at home looking after the kids."

"A fat lot of good you would be if you didn't have me here!" shouted a woman, who was lugging a heavy hose closer to the man.

"You're only a bloody nuisance!" screamed a man who was not the woman's husband.

The two men were about to have a punch-up, but Jeff parked himself between them.

"We have to deal with the fire," he said. "No time for this stuff."

Luckily, the two men calmed down and agreed, and did not exchange blows.

It was extremely hot and stressful fighting the fire. Tempers were frayed. The heavy protective clothing people were required to wear didn't make things easier. Sweat was pouring down all their bodies and they hardly ever stopped working for a drink of water. They were affected by smoke.

Rider and Axel reached home safely after sheltering from the fire in Tony's dam and the truck ride.

The change of weather did not last long and the hot wind from the west returned. There were still pockets of fire that had not been cleared up. The pockets were merging and burning towards Woogoo, and this fire directly threatened the township. So, measures were put in place to try and protect the people.

The fire progressed, burning along the north side of Woogoo and moving towards the ocean. More firefighters from the local community joined in to try and prevent any houses being burnt down. The fire was setting alight trees and grass on an area of parkland and was heading for the riding-school, where horses were stabled.

All the riding-school staff and many helpers were moving the horses out and leading them, by halter or bridle, down to the edge of the sea – a narrow strip of sand and pebbles next to the jetty. They were being lined up along the strip and the helpers, mainly children who rode them regularly, were to hold them by their reins there.

The people of Woogoo, at least on the north side, were being advised by police to leave their homes and proceed to the jetty, or to boats moored nearby, bringing life jackets if possible. If the fire reached the ocean, the people could jump into the water where it was shallow enough to stand and hold onto the posts supporting the jetty. If the fire was burning down the jetty, they should help one another make for the boats. At some point, the children holding the horses would have to abandon them and board the boats. The boats could sail farther out to sea, if necessary, and the horses would have to plunge into the water and swim for their lives.

Axel was one of the older children who went down to the jetty. People were just sitting around on it. They were shrouded in the thick smoke being blown in that direction, causing much coughing, sneezing, and rubbing of eyes.

Axel said to some folk near him, "It would be better to get into the water under the jetty."

Gradually, they did.

The owners of boats were now turning up and getting onto their boats, as they would want to protect the boats in the first instance. Axel was relieved to see them come, as they might have to offer space to people on and under the jetty and even help those who couldn't swim.

On the strip where the horses were lined up, there was much stamping of hooves, whinnying, and consternation. A little girl called Pieris offered to hold some of the horses. She had a calming effect on them. Nobody knew her in the riding-school. *Here is a new recruit to riding in the future,* the manager thought.

Axel told all this to Rider later. Rider was staying in her home as it was not threatened by the bushfire.

The fire by now had burnt through the parkland and the edges of the horse-riding premises and the motorbike club. The firefighters had managed to prevent any houses being burnt down. So, the fire had reached a caravan park where there were permanent residents. Some of these took shelter in the heavy concrete toilet and shower block. People on the jetty could see a conflagration of spot fires occurring in the caravan park, a tree here and there, and possibly a caravan, going up in smoke. One tree exploded.

Axel had dived into the water under the jetty. There, children were finding it difficult to hold onto the old timber posts while the ocean was sucking and pushing them backward and forwards. They got splinters in their hands. All were frightened and some were crying.

"You can hold onto my clothes," said Axel.

Other older children also did this for the younger ones. They were all bobbing and rocking in the ocean.

Some of the boats nosed up, and those on board dragged children out of the water and into the safety of the boat. Other people under the jetty were starting to swim for a boat if they could. On the strip with the horses, Pieris burst into tears. She handed the reins she was holding to another girl and ran into the water. Someone in a boat saw her and raced in, as fast as she could wade, to scoop her up and carry her back to the boat.

Suddenly, firefighters appeared on the edge of the caravan park where it met the coastal strip near the jetty. They were putting out a grassfire. The grass was very short. There was no chance of the fire reaching the jetty. This was the last shred of the fire.

As it turned out, the firefighters controlled and extinguished the fire before it burned down anything in Woogoo, except one caravan. The fire had finally been vanquished and everyone could go home and rest.

Rider's pigeon returned to its coop. It had taken it a long time, confused by all the smoke.

The weather was very hot before Christmas. Everybody lay low in their houses, trying to keep cool. At Jeff's place, there was little water in the garden and the vegetables were wilting and withering. Birds took refuge from the heat in the trees, where there were many insects to eat. Some birds fell out of the sky, dead. Whenever Jeff and Rider drove anywhere in the car, masses of grasshoppers flew into the windscreen and suicided by squashing themselves against the glass.

Jeff was exhausted after the firefighting. He was very tired and hardly ever made jokes anymore. He began making slippers from all the rabbit skins he had collected, as therapy. The fur would be on the inside. He said, "I will make some for Venetia, the doctor—"

"Don't make any for me," said Rider quickly. "I don't wear slippers."

"You know how I said I would have to mend and heal? That's what I'm doing because every time I put in a heel, I am having to mend the rabbit skin, as it is pulling out of the stitches."

Jeff was trying to be his jokey self again.

Rider and Jeff, together with Venetia and Katie, went into Woogoo to enjoy the annual celebrations of the founding of the town. Axel was going with another boy. Everyone knew they had to put on a fine show to bolster the morale of the townspeople after the fires. There was a gathering of poets and singers in the park and anyone could perform or sit on a folding chair and listen. They stood up, one after another, to recite or read the poems of Banjo Paterson, or recite their own poems, or sing their own songs, perhaps accompanying them with guitar or piano accordion.

At dusk, there was a special pony ride for children; they would ride their horses or ponies, riding-school or privately owned, through the streets of Woogoo. They took up the whole width of the road and were only lit by the Christmas lights with which houses were decorated as they passed them. Motorists drove slowly behind them.

Because it was nearly Christmas, on the front porch of many houses there were representations of Santa Claus or nativity scenes. These were homemade, using mops and brooms to make people's bodies and a frame for their clothing, gardening gloves and old shoes for their hands and feet, and small, round cushions to make a head with a face drawn on it. Rider and Jeff decided to judge which were the best ones. They gave their first prize to a Santa Claus who was dressed with a balaclava to look like a burglar stealing the presents – putting them *into* his sack. They liked the Santa who was sitting at a table enjoying a can of beer. They also liked a beautiful angel with a halo, dressed in a long, soft, white robe.

Rider said they used to have a similar annual event in her hometown.

No one had seen Gopher since the fire. Was he hiding somewhere, or had he lost his life in the fire? Perhaps it would never be known. But people were always waiting for him to pop out again, shocking a child. Someone had found out that he used to be a clown in a circus.

"Kangaroo Court"

One morning, Jeff said to Rider, "We must go to the public meeting in the community hall this Saturday about the bushfire. People will be jumping to all sorts of conclusions. It's especially important for you to have a say about this matter.

The meeting is being held to discuss how fighting the bushfire went. The important part of the discussion will be in determining what caused the fire. I think there will be a number of facts and theories about how the fire began."

When they went into the hall, Jeff and Rider chose seats towards the front. They were early and not many people had arrived yet. Rider noticed that some dignitaries were taking their seats on a stage in front of the audience. A little later, many more people had come and the meeting commenced.

The chairperson summarized the current situation at the beginning of the fire: "The fire was either started by a landowner who was burning off rubbish illegally, close to his boundary and a forested area; or a lightning strike in that same area. The police have collected evidence, and have been unable to decide which it was. The landowner has denied lighting a fire. It could have been begun by an unknown person."

Various representatives gave reports about the bushfire.

When the meeting was thrown open for discussion, a man put his hand up and said, "I think Gav started the fire."

Another man said, "The fire started from the old tip, and Gav was there."

Jeff immediately said, "I can answer that assertion."

Jeff explained there was nothing to link the fire at the tip to the fire on Brown Mountain. The tip was too far away. The fire brigade had poured water on the tip to keep that fire under control. He nudged Rider, "Your turn to talk."

Rider stood up. "I want to say something about Gav."

"You're his friend, aren't you? You wouldn't say anything against him," a person interjected.

"I am not his friend. I have just run into him a lot and got to know him well without choosing to. Gav says he didn't light the fire and I feel certain he didn't. He tells lies sometimes, but not very important ones. I saw Gav twice near to where the fire began, but then I bump into Gav all the time around the countryside. He's always snooping about. He was concerned about the fire and went back a second time."

"That's what the rogues do that light fires in the volunteers. They enjoy seeing the fires develop and go back to check they're still going."

"He's not one of them," continued Rider. "Everyone's biased against Gav because of the bullying they know about. He's not such a bad person, and he's also not such a good one. He's somewhere in the middle like lots of people in the fire brigade or the volunteers or anyone. But people don't like him because he's a bit strange, so they blame him for things which he didn't do."

"Isn't he a thief? Didn't he get into trouble with the police in Sydney?" another person shouted.

A council member asked a police officer to speak: "There are no complaints about Gav, and no charges have been laid against him."

Rider said, "He picks things up off the ground which people have dropped. We think he stole tools from our tool shed one night when we left it unlocked by accident. We didn't do anything about it, but we should have reported it to the police. Gav also dug things out of the tip, and kept a pile of junk nearby which he would repair and sell."

"Didn't Gav start a fire in the blackberries?" said someone. "He would do it again somewhere else."

A council member said, "The blackberries have been sprayed. People sometimes start fires in blackberries in order to force the council to spray them."

At this point, a man stood up and interrupted the meeting.

"I would like to say this: My family is extremely grateful to Gav. He found our son, Wolfe, in the reserve with an injured foot and carried him back to our place. We don't have any complaints about Gav and welcome him to our house any time."

The chairperson said that there should be a discussion about children entering the Brown Mountain reserve during the bushfire. This was to be deplored. Members of the audience had a lot to say on this subject.

After there were no more questions, the chairperson ended the meeting with the conclusion that the firefighters did the best they could and the community thanked them for all the work they did. There was no known loss of life. Some firefighters were recovering from smoke inhalation. One caravan was lost and the council had provided the owner with a new one. Some sheds were burnt. The eucalypt forest could regenerate.

As Jeff and Rider left the hall, they saw Gav in the back row. Probably he had been sitting there silently from the beginning.

They heard later that Gav and Wolfe had formed a bond because both of them had been teased about their names at school. The children had made howling noises at Wolfe. Gav had been teased about his true name, which was a family name, Gaviston. Teachers always know what your proper name is, and then all the kids do.

Rider said to Jeff, "Gav objected to my being called Rider, and look at what *his* name is. I always thought his name was Gavin."

Wolfe's parents were trying to help Gav's family, especially the child who needed his kidney replaced. They were raising funds from the community for a kidney transplant for him. There were hopes that Gav would grow up to fit into the community, neither as a particularly good person nor a bad one.

Jeff said, "There's a chance Gav would get a job with the fire brigade. They would understand him but would give him a hard time if he behaved badly. Or he might do well as an ambulance officer, or in the rescue services. They tend to dislike having to work with women."

"Gav doesn't dislike women," Rider replied, not seeing the distinction.

Jeff said, "Well, I don't know what Gav's relations with women would be like." He then ventured an opinion, "I think he would like women to be almost angelic."

"To make up for his faults?"

"Something like that. But Rider, the police haven't necessarily finished with Gav yet. They will still be investigating whether he lit the fire or other possible misdemeanours."

Jeff and Rider also heard that Bruno the Brazilian, who had not attended the meeting, had helped fight the fires. He had moved his family to Woogoo for a while because of the fire danger and then back to their house in the bush. Jeff and Rider walked there one day to say hello to them. They had meant to do it earlier.

One day, Jeff heard someone knocking on the door of his house. *This person has crept up on me quietly*, he thought. He opened the door. It was a policeman.

"Are you Jeffrey Milgate?" he said.

"Yes."

"We believe that a girl called Saskia Rider Smith is staying in your house."

"That is true," said Jeff, heaving a sigh. "She's not here at the moment. I didn't know her surname was Smith."

"Her mother has been searching for her for quite some time. She registered her daughter as missing with the police. This girl is only aged fourteen."

"Quite so," said Jeff. "She told me she was almost fifteen and was looking for a job when she came here, but I never heard about her having a birthday. I tried to find her work and let her stay here rather than travelling and getting into strife. I made her write letters to her mother to assure her of her daughter's safety. But she would not tell me her mother's name and address."

"Her mother was very worried and enlisted the help of the police to find her. The law doesn't regard the girl as being safe in your care. She is underage and should be with her mother, or have her mother's permission to be here. You are to come to the police station in Woogoo as soon as possible, with Saskia, to answer questions."

"Can I bring a female friend to vouch for my good character?"

"Yes, but the police may insist on interviewing the three of you separately. Saskia will be interviewed by a social worker as well. The mother will be required to identify Saskia when that can be arranged."

When Rider came home, Jeff said, "We are in deep trouble with the police. They have found out who you are. We are ordered to go to the police station."

The police booked an appointment for Jeff, Venetia, and Rider to attend at the police station. The police took down a statement from Jeff about his offering Rider bed and board in return for part-time work on his property. Jeff said he didn't know her full name and address, and couldn't contact her mother. He had asked her to write letters to her mother and she had written several. He saw her post them. Rider said all that was true.

Venetia said she was a friend of Jeff's and he was a good bloke, a volunteer firefighter, and a respected member of the community. Rider had been welcomed at her place, and she thought she was a happy girl and a resilient person. The police said they would contact Rider's mother again and advise her to come and see her daughter. Jeff was not to prevent this. Rider had a session with the social worker, who said Rider did not have any appreciable problems.

At this time, the police issued a public warning about kidnappers: Children were to be told never to take lifts in cars or on motorbikes with people they didn't know. Children shouldn't accept lollies from people, or drinks in a bar from a stranger if they were older children. Lollies and drinks could be spiked with drugs that made you sleepy and vulnerable. The situation was bad in Sydney because police were having to look for so many missing children who had been locked up to work in the illegal drug trade. Some attempts had been made to kidnap children in and around Woogoo, but they had been unsuccessful so far. This situation might change.

People were saying, "Will it change for the better, or worse?"

Rider's Mother Visits

Rider and Jeff had a quiet Christmas season. There was a smoke or dust haze everywhere. At Jeff's waterhole, where there was barely a trickle of water, the echidna had given birth to a baby from the egg in her pouch. She would walk to the chook yard and poke her long snout through the chicken wire to drink the chickens' water. She reared and nurtured the little puggle while it was growing its spines. Now, it no longer needed its mother – its father had gone away long ago after mating. Rider and Jeff saw the almost grownup puggle out foraging for ants.

Rider had lost touch for a while with Tony and Axel. They would all meet up later when Tech college started again. She hoped they would still be her friends.

Jeff suggested to Rider that she should phone her mother and ask her to come and visit. Rider had written her a few letters, and Jeff had been in touch with her.

"What will she say to me?" said Rider, in alarm. Jeff had no answer, but they decided between them that she should phone on Christmas Day when her mother was sure to be pleasant to her.

"Invite her to stay here on your birthday, which is only three weeks away," said Jeff. "She will be pleased to see you on your birthday."

Rider plucked up the courage to phone. "Hello, Mum. I'm afraid you haven't seen me for a long time," she said, screwing up her face in anxiety. "How are you?"

"Saskia! Thank you for all your letters. Are you well?"

"Yes thanks, Mum. I am living at Jeff's house. Would you visit us on my birthday?"

"Of course, I'd like to come and see you, Sassy. I've missed you so much."

"I've missed you too, Mum."

"If you give me the address, my battered old car can just about get me there."

Rider told her the address and they spoke a few more words. Nothing terrible happened.

"She's coming here, and she calls me Sassy," Rider said to Jeff. "I feel so embarrassed."

"Isn't that what she always called you?"

"Yes. My name was Saskia Smith. But I don't want to be Sassy now." She was kicking the leg of the chair.

"Well, on your birthday make a formal announcement that your name is Rider from then on."

Because it was Christmas Day, Jeff had a present for Rider, which was for her birthday too. He took her out to the shed, and there it was, gleaming and glinting in the dusty light: a solar-powered motorbike.

"Oh, thank you, Jeff!"

"You can't ride it on public roads for another year. You can only ride it around the block."

Rider went off to try out the bike immediately, with the dogs barking and chasing after her.

Later in the day, Rider asked Jeff about his relationship with a lady who used to be charming to him at the fishing jetty. (She was really thinking about her mother's boyfriend.) Jeff said they were just being social and chatty, and he hadn't developed an attraction to her. Another lady friend had desired a relationship with him once after his wife died, and she wanted to come and live with him. But he felt too old for it. He had loved his wife.

"When she died, I enjoyed my freedom. People like their independence too. But Venetia...Venetia..." Jeff's voice trailed off. He dropped the knife he was polishing on the floor. "She's so much younger than I am."

"Oh yes. But do you think my mother neglected me when she went off with her boyfriend?"

"A little. She was having some fun in her life."

On her birthday, Rider was pleased to have reached fifteen years at last. She felt older and more mature. In the mirror, she saw that she was taller and bigger than she had ever been. She still had her typical haircut and clothes, but a slightly feminine outline.

Her mother arrived in the afternoon, after starting early in the morning, wearing one of the nice dresses she made. Rider thought her fair hair was greyer, and she looked smaller and thinner. Rider ran forward and put her arms around her mother. She didn't know she was going to do that. She didn't know what to say.

She blurted out, choking on the words, "I love you, Mum, I always loved you, but I was so selfish."

"I love you too Saskia, in spite of everything," Mum said. "And I see you've grown a lot."

Jeff came out of the house to greet her. She said her name was Lilian.

"You are very welcome," said Jeff. "Please make yourself at home."

Everyone felt awkward. Mum brought in her bags to the bedroom and excused herself to use the bathroom while Jeff made tea. It was good weather for sitting at the outdoor table.

"It's a nice place you have here, Jeff," she said, settling herself in a chair.

"Yes, it is."

In the background were the sounds of nature: a bird, a frog, a cricket. The teacups clinked. Breaths were bated.

Plunging in the deep end, Rider said in strained tones, "I'm sorry, Mum, for running away."

Mum put down her cup. Her mind was released. "I was terribly worried because I didn't know anything about where you had gone for days. I reported you as missing to the police straight away. I began driving around the roads and so did the police, but no one spotted you. I expected to hear of a dreadful accident or crime, and it was the worst experience of my life. When your letter arrived, I was relieved, though I couldn't be sure that you really were all right. Then I felt cross because I couldn't get in touch with you. Why did you do this, Sassy?"

Rider cringed. She was close to tears, but she couldn't cry.

"I felt lonely when Peter suddenly left home without telling us. You often stayed away from home at night with your boyfriend, but I had Peter as a companion in the house. Then no one was there."

"I offered to take you with me, but you wouldn't come."

"I know."

"I've broken up with that man. Peter contacted me later with his address." She was weeping noiselessly, dabbing her face with a tissue. "I'm so glad to see you."

That was the thing nearest to her heart. They all fell to munching Jeff's biscuits.

"What are you going to do now?" Mum asked Rider.

"I want to stay with Jeff and go to the Tech. college in Woogoo," said Rider. "Jeff is like a father to me." Her voice choked with emotion. "I never had a father."

"I don't know what happened to your father."

"It doesn't matter anymore."

"I've brought you a hammer your dad left behind, which has his name cut into the handle. If you ever go in search of him, you can take it as proof that you are his daughter."

She went to her car to get the hammer, brought it back, and handed it to Rider. Rider read out her father's name: "Euie Smith."

Jeff said, "I'm happy for Rider to remain here. I always said it was her home as long as she wanted. She has grown up about two years, in one year."

Now Mum cried. She had found her daughter but had lost her. She'd made a new life with Jeff. She thought this would happen.

"I will come and visit you," said Rider. "I'm having such an exciting time with Jeff."

"Exciting! Why, what are you doing?"

"I mean playing with the dogs, being with my friends, going camping in the bush, and going to the beach – all that kind of thing."

Mum nodded and reached out across the table to squeeze Rider's arm while she regained her composure.

"I'm on your side, Sassy. The fact is, there are few opportunities for the young where I live, no technical college. A lot of them drift away."

Rider spent time alone with Mum and showed her all the things she did at Jeff's place. She had a display of the wooden toys Jeff taught her to make. She told Mum about correspondence school and her friends. She said she was called Rider now.

Mum said, "I will call you Saskia, which sounds more grownup."

"I'll tell other people my name is Saskia Rider, but only my mother calls me Saskia."

When Jeff had a chance to talk with Mum, he told her how his wife had died and the rest of his family had gone to live in Greenland. Then he described to her all he knew about Rider's travels and her life at Woogoo.

Rider had tears in her eyes when she said goodbye to her mum the next morning. She was relieved that she wasn't angry with her and she could imagine, more clearly, how Mum felt when she ran away from home. She wished Mum hadn't cried so much. Mum told her how much she loved her, and would always love her because she was her daughter.

"I'm going to phone Mum now and again when I have something interesting to tell her," Rider said to Jeff afterward. "And see her more often. When I'm older and more mature, I'll try to find my father."

A Birthday Party and Riding with a Dolphin

Rider was sitting outside when she saw two magpies under a tree. One was lying on its back with the other on top; then they rolled over and changed places while nipping and clawing each other and flapping their wings.

"Are these magpies fighting, mating, or playing?" she asked Jeff, who was out in the garden with a pot of cooking water to empty onto a plant. He watched them.

"I'd say playing."

"I agree. I've grown rather fond of birds. It's helping me think about flying machines."

"Look! Now there's a baby walking over."

The baby magpie, appearing to be bigger than its parents because of its extra grey, soft chest feathers, was squawking loudly for food.

Rider said, "I've been giving the magpies dried dogfood to eat, on the sundial. They love it. They know I put it out for them and sing their thanks to me while I'm close by. When I opened the door one morning, two baby magpies flew over to the door, squawking at me for food. They had their eyes on the door all the time. After that, one of them was sitting on the doormat every morning, and I almost trod on it. No other birds are as smart."

"Oh, I see," said Jeff. "Well then, may I ask what you want to do for your birthday?"

"I'll tell you later."

Rider reckoned she would have a small party for her fifteenth birthday. *I might have a treasure hunt*, she thought.

She paid a visit to the cow and the sheep to see if they had any helpful suggestions, as they were part of her life. She decided to decorate them with garlands of flowers and leaves. She spent some time learning to make the garlands, weaving the plants together into necklaces. When she put them on Yak and Ivana, they tried to eat them.

I should have known it.

Yak went up to the fence and began rubbing her garland off against the wires. Rider ran to her saying, "No, Yak, no!" and interposed herself between the cow and the fence. She accidentally left the gate open and Ivana dashed out straight away and ran into the vegetable garden. She seemed to know exactly where it was. She was already eating the vegetables voraciously when Rider caught up with her. Then, Ivana led her a chase around all the vegies, trampling them down as she went on her merry way. Rider could not grab her and had to get the help of Barker and Pogo, who were in the house. They had a difficult time of it, too, before they could finally induce Ivana to go back into the paddock. She was a taskmaster at dodging quickly to the left or to the right, just as you thought you had her cornered and within your grasp.

"You've had your fun!" shouted Rider to Yak and Ivana, as she returned to the house.

After the escapade of the animals, Rider went around to Venetia and Katie's places to invite them to her party. So now the party was truly happening. When she got home again, she remembered to tell Jeff about it.

Rider walked into Woogoo to invite Axel and Tony. Rider and Axel would soon be going to the Tech college in Woogoo where Tony was studying already.

"Have you decided what to do at Tech college yet?" Rider asked Axel.

"No, but I'm concerned about the uncertainty for young people in education, work, and ability to earn," replied Axel.

Axel wasn't fifteen yet, but he had completed his correspondence courses. He was a thoughtful person and had become more preoccupied and introspective since the fire. But he was still grappling with these large subjects and did not seem to have anything else to say about them.

Rider walked around to Tony's digs and asked him about his Tech college course.

"I'm studying environmental science," Tony said. "Like wind and wave power, and building houses completely from waste material. I'm very committed to it."

He described the wind generator he had made from junk, which was producing electricity for his home.

"I'll be keen to learn something that Jeff doesn't know," said Rider. "Like building and driving spaceships."

Both the boys said they'd see more of Rider again when they all went to Tech.

On the day of the party, Venetia brought a scrumptious chocolate cake, with cream in the middle, chocolate icing, and nuts. All and sundry felt at home running about Jeff's place on a treasure hunt, where they discovered Rider's fantastic motorbike.

The treasure hunt had to be where the dogs couldn't go. One of the clues was "Food lies in a tree, how happy you'll be." The guests climbed and searched the food trees for the next clue, which was "A tisket, a tasket, what you need is a basket." But where was the basket? No sign of one. Rider and Jeff had made round fishing baskets out of dried reeds as presents for everyone and they had piled them high on the roof to look like a chimney. Before long, Tony caught sight of it and mounted a ladder to toss the baskets down. There was another clue, "Where your treasure is, there will your heart be also." Nobody could solve this one until they began opening up cupboards all around the house. The treasure, a box of sweets, was in the fridge with a bull's heart. The heart was a treat for the dogs.

Everybody shared the sweets. Katie tipped her fishing basket upside down and stuffed her head in the opening, saying, "Look, I'm a spacewoman." Tony said he would put his dirty clothes for one week in his basket, as a laundry basket. Others generally murmured, "That's not many dirty clothes for a week."

Jeff cut the heart in half for the two dogs.

"Now Barker and Pogo, have a heart," he said, setting their bowls on the floor. "Don't be half-hearted with your lot."

The dogs weren't listening; they were eating to their heart's content.

Rider took the left-over food to Yak and Ivana. They ate it all up.

Rider had something she wanted to do in the way of a holiday treat. It was to ride with the dolphins. She often saw the fisherman, Oscar, at the markets, and Rider knew that Oscar would take people out in his fishing boat to ride with dolphins. Some of these dolphins were the same ones that came to the jetty to be petted by people. They were partly tame.

"Would you be able one day to take me out to ride with the dolphins?" she asked Oscar.

"I could. There have been a lot of sightings of dolphins lately. Or whales. It's the time of year for them. We'll be catching fish at the time and you could help."

Rider boarded the fishing boat with a small cloth satchel of belongings. The boat chugged out of the harbour. Oscar was going to teach her all the jobs on the boat, as they netted fish.

Out in the open sea, it was rougher, with grey waves and weather. In the afternoon, the sun broke through the clouds and sparkled on the wave tops. Then, a pod of dolphins appeared at the side of the boat, but a little farther back in the wake. They rose in a curve together above the waves before disappearing again.

Oscar had a life jacket and a harness ready for Rider to put on, with a long rope attached. He knew what to do next.

"Quick, jump in the water and when they rise, ride with a dolphin while they are following the boat. Swim to the nearest one, put your arm over it and hold the flipper on the other side."

The boat was slowed while Rider leaped in the direction of the dolphins, knowing the crew could haul her back in. The dolphins surfaced again and she managed to hold onto the nearest one. The dolphins swam on the surface for a while and Rider went with them. Then, they plunged down in the water and forced her to let go.

As Rider climbed onto the deck, the men were clapping and cheering. They knew how wonderful it was to swim with dolphins since they had done it too, when young.

Going on down the coast, Rider had to strain at the nets with might and main. The crew pulled in a good load of fish. When they were gliding in on smoother waters to the jetty at Woogoo, Oscar said he couldn't see Jeff there to meet her.

"That's because I'm giving him a surprise."

She was going to take him a satchel full of fish, but that wasn't the real reason. She didn't want Jeff to meet Oscar and find out about the dolphin ride.

The next morning, Jeff and Rider read in the paper that a girl had been kidnapped on the street in Woogoo in the evening.

"Youngsters shouldn't walk around on their own after dark," said Jeff.

"Why didn't she scream for help?"

"They would have gagged her, or made her unconscious by forcing her to sniff chloroform."

"What will happen now?"

"The police will look for her until they find her. They are getting to grips more and more with this drug trade situation."

Ninety-Mile Beach

One day, Jeff and Rider went fishing from the jetty. It was a lovely day, with a light sea breeze. They unpacked and set up their gear and threw out their lines.

They turned to discussing the hole in society, which they had talked about before, and other topics. Rider said, "Why did many people go to live in Greenland, when it was expensive, and leave a hole in our society?"

"The government supported it because it was too hot in Australia and we were over-populated, putting pressure on the environment. Also, it held out hope for the future when Earth could no longer sustain human life. And sometimes, humans mistakenly do things just because they can."

"Did people ever have a hole in society in the past?"

"Yes, when they had migration, wars, or diseases, I think."

Rider said she was worried about the lies she told. She had pretended to be a boy and lied about her age, and invented an uncle that she didn't have. She had said she was called Rider, and she told things about her mum which weren't true.

"Those are white lies," said Jeff. "People occasionally need them to get by in life. But what about how you treated your mother by leaving home without telling her? She would have been worried stiff until she had a note from you, and then anxious still. Your mother's a nice person and she didn't deserve it. Did you notice how much she cried when she came to visit? She was working off all her stress."

By this time, they had caught enough fish for at least two days, and they agreed to pack up and go home.

Later, weary from the day's activities, Rider went to lie down in her room. She reminded herself of what she'd been through in the past year and wondered if she'd ever be the same again. She'd missed a lot of regular school, simply because she thought the school authorities would send her back to Mum. She couldn't think why she had been so much against Mum.

She hadn't completed correspondence school, but she had a chance to make up for it at the Tech college. She had the support of Jeff, who was a real friend, guardian, and mentor. She would be able to make something out of her life. She could hold on.

Before going to bed that night, she said to Jeff, "Perhaps your house was named Endeavour because it meant trying hard to do things, being patient, and not giving up."

"It might have been."

"You know, you used to joke so much, and now you don't any more. You're too serious."

"I expect I will be inspired again someday. I've been a bit depressed lately."

Jeff felt he had put Rider in harm's way. Apparently, his small endeavours in joking had either fallen flat or on deaf ears.

"Why is there a difference between Sydney, Woogoo, and the small inland country town I grew up in?" said Rider. "Young people can't get work in Sydney; they can in Woogoo, but not in a small country town."

"Woogoo is thriving. The land is rich and fertile for farming, and the sea provides a ready income. It has bushland and natural beauty. It, and other towns along the coast, are the best places to live. The air is clean, and they are also holiday destinations," said Jeff. "Do you think we are living a good life here, on the whole, or a poor life?"

"A good life."

"And is that a rich life? I mean, with healthy food, happiness, and one as fine as wealthy people could pay for, or better."

"Yes."

Jeff said, "Our lifestyle has been chosen by people, in their small and imperfect ways, even in big cities, to better the lives of all who live in the world. It is based on books like 'How to Avoid the Food Shortage'."

"Would I have to read the books?"

"No, because you are learning the lifestyle from everyone as you grow up."

Jeff didn't want Rider to read on this subject when she had enough to do getting through her curriculum. He thought it would be a wise plan for him and Rider to take a holiday. It would just fit in before Tech college started. They would go to a sandy beach, as it was what Rider always desired. It would have to be one where lots happened.

Because Jeff had repaired fences for him, his next-door neighbour said he would milk the cow and tend to the chickens while they were away. It would be better to leave the animals on the place as if someone was there. They would let the pigeons fly about freely to fend for themselves by opening the feed door. Katie offered to care for Barker and Pogo.

Rider was very excited. They heard from people about the ninety-mile beach in the state of Victoria. You could swim and surf, ride motorbikes on the beach, and do hang-gliding.

"We don't have a surfboard," said Rider.

"Never mind. We'll go there and see what we can hire."

They would pack a tent, a folding table, and chairs, and tie the motorbike to the roof rack. Jeff was going to include his carpentry tools, hoping he would need them for something.

They drove south along the continuation of the coast road, through farmland and bushland and small coastal towns. Sometimes, they saw bush fires and grass fires, but the road wasn't ever cut by fire. Jeff complained as usual about the potholes and said that the trucking companies would have to club together and fill them in.

Late in the day, they arrived at the beach. They ran down the sand to the Southern Ocean which goes all the way to Antarctica. There was a cool wind blowing behind the surf. Seagulls called out with shrill cries, circling overhead. It was exhilarating.

They put up their tent in the partly cleared edge of the beach, where low-growing coastal shrubs provided shelter from the wind.

"Quick, help me get the motorbike off the roof rack," said Rider impatiently, tugging at Jeff's arm.

Soon, she was riding up and down the hard sand in the middle of the beach, while Jeff unfolded the table and chairs and was preparing a meal on a small stove with the food they had brought. That was where the setting sun shone on them as they ate their dinner at dusk and crawled into their sleeping bags.

In the morning, there were some young people on the beach. They had come with their surfboards to find the best spot for surfing that day. Rider went to join them in the surf, and in no time, she was talking with them. They lent her a spare surfboard. Jeff, who was still finishing his breakfast, watched Rider's first clumsy attempts to use the surfboard and chuckled to himself when she fell off it, splashing into the sea.

Rider followed the surfers out to where they were catching waves. She had to face the shore lying on the board, and paddle like mad or she would miss the wave. She was stretched to her limit. When she had caught the wave, she had to stand up quickly on the board and keep her balance at the same time. Almost impossible! If she could reach the shore pointing straight to it, it was enough – "Weeeee!" There was the speed, the feeling of weightlessness and freedom, effortlessly gliding through the water.

Later in the day, Jeff and Rider were instructed to change their camping site to the official camping ground, with earth toilets and water tanks. Rider was able to hire a surfboard there. Jeff had no wish to be swimming and surfing.

Near to the camping ground, Jeff noticed a cluster of old beach houses that were derelict and unoccupied. They could be repaired, but people had been removing the timber that was falling off them. Jeff decided to begin restoring one that was in a better condition, using timber that was nearly dropping off the worst houses. He was happy to have a use for his carpentry tools and he had even brought a fold-up ladder.

Nobody paid much attention to Jeff repairing the house. As it progressed, Rider came to help now and again. After the floor was made stable, Jeff bought a tin of white paint and painted on a completed wall of the house, *Ninety-Mile Beach Clubhouse*. People then noticed the house.

"You've been rebuilding this house for the use of the community here," said a man. "Good on you."

"We approve of what you've done," said the couple who ran the camping ground. "These houses have been falling apart for years. People steal the timber, and few owners ever show up."

Jeff said he thought the community should sometimes have a slightly better shelter than their tents and could meet here to talk together or have a party.

While Jeff was engaged with his house repairs, Rider was improving her surfboard riding skills, and giving some of the youngsters turns at riding her motorbike on the beach. Rider was interested in doing hang-gliding and Jeff was willing to pay for her to have some training sessions that were available. Later, he didn't have to pay, because of his rebuilding of the house for the community's clubhouse.

Rider loved the feeling of hang-gliding through the air over the landscape, flying exposed to the elements like a bird. Wearing a harness and holding the control bar on a frame, she would begin by running so that the wing would take to the air. After take-off, she would gently soar. She could feel the wind rushing past and see the ground race away beneath her. Sitting, standing, or leaning forward, and using her whole body to propel herself upwards or turn left and right, she was always held aloft by the wing above, until she wanted to float to the ground again. It was breath-taking.

Rider and Jeff went shopping for food almost every day at the local village. One day, a girl was bitten by a venomous spider. Rider was filled with admiration for the girl, Bridget, when she got to know her better on taking her to the local hospital. Jeff had put a firm bandage around her leg in the place where the bite was, and he and Rider rushed her to the nearest small town for an injection of anti-venom. Bridget started to lose consciousness in the car, and Jeff and Rider had to support her, one on each side, into the emergency ward. While Jeff was booking her in, Rider sat beside Bridget and kept talking to her to keep her awake.

"Don't fall asleep, Bridget. Tell me what you did for Christmas."

"Oh, I went to see my granny and tried on her funny old-fashioned dresses. Everyone laughed at me, except granny." Bridget's speech was slurred.

Jeff returned with a glass of water; she drank it and revived a little. Soon, it was her turn to see the doctor. She recovered well after treatment.

Bridget was friends with another girl, Ally. They stuck together but were very independent. They liked surfing. They often came to the clubhouse for more protection from the weather than they had in the rather small tent they shared. Jeff was always concerned about the girls. Rider was attracted to the clubhouse if the girls were there. They were about her age. If they brought their radio, all three of them would dance about to the music.

Rider and the girls found some sand dunes. It took a vigorous effort to run up them, feet and toes digging and clawing into the sand. Then they ran down the hills, sinking ever lower in the sand until they fell over and rolled and tumbled to the bottom. They all laughed and giggled, shaking the sand out of their clothes and hair.

Jeff had joined a group who were fishing off some rocks round at a headland. It was known as the prime place to catch fish. So, he and Rider often ate fish. Rider actually managed to catch a rabbit. Bridget and some girls screamed when they saw her wring its neck. She realized, as a consequence, that she wouldn't like to kill anything in front of girls in the future. They wouldn't understand her bush training. But she skinned and cleaned the rabbit and cooked it with seaweed for a dinner party.

Everybody sat outside on the grass and looked at the Southern Cross which guided mariners of old, the Milky Way, and the stars as they came out. Jeff said the stars commemorated all beginnings of life.

After three weeks at Ninety-Mile Beach, it was time to go home. Jeff and Rider's legacy to the beach community was the clubhouse they made, which everyone could share. That is until someone turned up to claim the house, which wasn't likely.

Rider persuaded Jeff to take a free ride on the hang-glider before going, as a reward for his work. Jeff thoroughly enjoyed it.

"It gives a lift to my spirits," he said.

Loading their gear into the car, Rider was feeling sad. It had been a wonderful holiday.

"Couldn't we return soon? We don't have to live at Woogoo all the time."

"We'll come back in your next holidays from the Tech college. You'll have earned a surfboard by then. In the winter vacation, it would be best if you went and stayed with your mother. She said she wanted you to help her move furniture. She would like to make you some dresses and have conversations with you."

On the way home, Rider talked about how she aspired to become proficient at hang-gliding and to go sky-surfing on the Morning Glory in Queensland. The Morning Glory was a sequence of roll clouds that occurred thousands of feet above the ground, which hang-gliders could reach by catching thermals or updrafts it created, and then surf the clouds.

"I'd like to make solar-powered wings that you could strap on and fly with. I'll call them *Dragonfly* in remembrance of the dragon I had in a dream. I'll have to do research on birds."

"Do you mean you'd flap the wings with your arms?"

"No, the solar power would operate the wings through a mechanical device. But the person could control direction with their body."

"I think it would be possible. But imagine all the children who'd like to fly about on wings. They'd say to their parents, 'Goodbye, I'm off flying for the day. See you later,' and off they'd go. The parents wouldn't know where they were and they could be in danger of having accidents."

"I think it would be awesome. The children would love it. There will have to be a special place where they can go and fly."

Rider and Jeff continued on their way, anticipating a bright future achieving their hopes and dreams, with visits to Mum and to the beach.

If you run away from home, you might have a bad time, but it worked for Rider.

www.ingramcontent.com/pod-product-compliance
Lightning Source LLC
Chambersburg PA
CBHW061514050726
47593CB00002B/566